SCIENCE
SQUAD

Runway ZomBee

A Zombie Bee Hunter's Journal

Book design by Jake Slavik
Illustrations by Arpad Olbey

Photograph Page 187: Core A, Runckel C, Ivers J, Quock C, Siapno T, et al. (2012). "A new threat to honey bees, the parasitic phorid fly *Apocephalus borealis*". PLoS ONE 7 (1). DOI:10.1371/journal.pone.0029639.

Design Elements: Shutterstock Images

Published in the United States by Jolly Fish Press, an imprint of North Star Editions, Inc.

First Edition
First Printing, 2018

This is a work of fiction. Names, characters, places, and incidents are either the product of the author's imagination or are used fictitiously, and any resemblance to actual persons living or dead, business establishments, events, or locales is entirely coincidental.

Library of Congress Cataloging-in-Publication Data (pending)
978-1-63163-165-8 (paperback)
978-1-63163-164-1 (hardcover)

Jolly Fish Press
North Star Editions, Inc.
2297 Waters Drive
Mendota Heights, MN 55120
www.jollyfishpress.com

Printed in the United States of America

Runway ZomBee

A Zombie Bee Hunter's Journal

by J. A. Watson

Illustrations by Arpad Olbey | Text by Amanda Humann

JOLLY FiSH PRESS

Mendota Heights, Minnesota

First Wednesday
of Summer, Part 1

It was *so* not my fault that my arm got stuck in the mailbox at the top of the hill.

I thought I could retrieve the Science Squad summer confirmation form. I mean, I'd mailed it only *hours* before. I reached in the opening and fished around, but I couldn't feel ANYTHING. When I tried to pull my hand out, the door snapped shut and got stuck on my chunky, oversized ring. It's the one that Hannah (I mean Moondew) gave me. It has the mini globe on top with glow-in-the-dark bees floating inside. It went really well with my turquoise top, which was important, because I still believe in making an effort to look decent—even if I'm just going to the mailbox. It keeps me from being a completely socially unredeemable nerd.

I think.

Then again, I suppose it might be considered nerdy to desperately grip the mailbox with both legs and the free arm, heaving and grunting like a deranged, sweaty bear trying to get its paw out of a metal beehive.

No amount of fashion know-how can save that.

hand and cute bee ring stuck in here

imagine this filled with honey!

Who decided to make those openings so narrow and not-arm-shaped, anyway?

Luckily, the street was empty, so no one saw me. I gave up pulling on my arm and stood there roasting under the sun for ~~hours~~ minutes (but it felt like hours) with my hand stuck in that mailbox prison. Rain clouds approached from the coast. Typical San Francisco weather—just can't make up its mind. Sun, rain, sun, rain. Fog. Rain.

I know how it feels.

Note to science self:

When you go to the mailbox at the top of the hill, make sure that you really want to put that mail in there, 'cause there's no getting it back out.

Unless what you put in the mailbox is a body part.

That is still attached to you.

And you are lucky, 'cause the mailman comes back down the hill to deliver mail on the other side of the street, and after laughing *hysterically* at your plight until his eyes water, he gives you a lecture on federal offenses and the mail, etc. Then he helps you get your arm (and only your arm) out. And then he starts laughing again.

And then it rains.

Note to fashion self:

Wear smaller jewelry on hands. Save the "statement piece" accessories for days when you won't be cramming your hands down the throat of an angry mailbox.

I just realized that I'm jumping ahead writing this down, 'cause I haven't written anything in here for a long time.

RAKSHA KUMAR'S SUMMER TO-DO LIST:

1. Journal: Catch up!

Catch Up: Last Week of School

I haven't been very good at writing much in my field journal/sketchbook, because the end of the school year was *so* crazy. Why do teachers pile up all the big deadlines and due dates for the end of the year, when all kids can think about is summer? Do they get some kind of *bonus* for every kid they fail? I'm not worried about failing, but I still feel the pain of piles of stuff at the end of the year. Work is work, regardless of how smart you are.

Every teacher piles it on, even in PE! We had to run a whole mile outside in eighty-four-degree heat because San Francisco got a freak heat wave the same day Mr. Mitzel decided to give us our PE "final." At least all we had to do was complete the mile and not be the last to cross the finish line. The only things that kept me and ~~Hannah~~ Moondew moving were talking about Science Squad and making sure we stayed ahead of

Abby Grayner so we wouldn't be last over the line. Her asthma was acting up, so it was easy. My fashion brain examined the way she had tied her PE shirt off to the side—not a bad way to deal with an overly large top— and my science brain worried if she would be okay. It was so hot, and that *can't* be easy with asthma. Then my feet told both of my brains to shut the heck up and keep moving.

"I'm guessing Mari freaked when she realized that our final badge project for the Squad was collaborative," said Moondew (yay! I remembered Hannah's latest "natural name") as we ~~ran~~ shuffled along the track outside our school. "That girl really needs to mellow out. All her stress is bad for the universe."

Oh, and in case future me is reading this and can't remember who Mari is, this is *NOT* Mari from sixth grade English class. This is Science Squad *archnemesis* Mari Gonzalez. She may go to a different school than us, but she's still a part of our weekly life. I know I promised two years ago to stop writing about how annoying she is because it seems stupid to fill my journal with notes about *her.* But it's been four years since we all joined the Squad, and she hasn't changed since day one. She's still trying to outshine everyone (especially me) on the Squad and still brings a general level of know-it-all-ness to our meetings. The other kids (the only ones left are Quiet Kenny and The Twins) don't seem to care, but she still drives me and Moondew *NUTS.* I'm SO glad we are at the last level and graduating. I'll miss the science but not my weekly doses of Mari.

"Yeah, I'm sure she's truly thrilled to share the spotlight with everyone," I said. "I bet she nominates herself to be in charge before we even bring out the donuts in the next meeting. Ooh, donuts. Let's stop by Nuts for Dough after school."

"Okay, and let's try those new unicorn tea drinks, too," said Moondew, panting. "We totally deserve one after this, and then I can do a review for my tea channel."

"Maybe Mari'll give herself a better title than 'Captain' or 'President' this time. She really should show some creativity," I said, wiping the sweat off my forehead. "Hey, I have the perfect name for her. She should be called 'Her Royal Majesty the Queen Bee' since we're doing bee science. That way, we can insist that she only eats those gross jelly donuts, since all queen bees eat is royal jelly."

"I see you are already one with the bees and their info," said Moondew. "That's so Zen of you."

It's true. The moment Ms. Char (still our Science Squad sponsor and awesome science teacher) said a possible final project would be to "hunt zombies," I read *everything* I could find on the Internet about them. Waste of time. We aren't studying human zombies. But we ARE studying *real* zombies. When she finally gave us a packet on the Zombie Bee (ZomBee, get it?) Project, I plowed through it for interesting information like a tourist searching for souvenirs in Chinatown.

I haven't gone crazy or anything like that, but I was *really* disappointed to learn that the zombie bees don't eat each other's brains. I'd pictured them flying loops and crooked paths. And instead of buzzing, I was thinking they'd make a sound that sounded like *brainzzzz* . . .

This is what actually happens:

What I Imagined:

brainzzzzz

VS

What Actually Happens:

Zombie fly lays eggs in a bee
1.

Eggs hatch into larvae and eat their host
2.

Larvae burst out, become pupae
3.

The pupae then become adults
4.

Our job will be to find bees who may be infected with parasites by building bee-attracting lights, then collecting the bees as samples and watching them for signs of infection. Then we report what we found to the scientists who are studying the bees. We actually get to be a part of real science! No exploding Mentos in bottles of cola (although that is pretty cool) or making baking soda volcanoes—we're doing *REAL* science!

13

Anyway, back to our conversation at school:

"I'm surprised that Mari voted for the creepiest, crawliest project for our last badge," I said. "I mean, remember how she reacted when we dissected squid at the aquarium? I'm pretty sure they automatically hand out barf bags with that experiment now, all because of her."

I'm surprised Mari stuck with the Squad after that, 'cause I expected that public puking in an aquarium trash can would have dulled her enthusiasm, but no. She's like a bad rash—she keeps coming back.

"Maybe she's over her obsession with engineering and building stuff, and she wants to switch to living things," said Moondew.

"Yeah, right, and the sky is bright yellow, gravity doesn't exist, and you hate rocks. Come to think of it, Ms. 'Geology Rocks!,' why did you vote for the bee project when one of our choices was helping on that fossil dig?"

"Eh. I helped on that exact same site last year during spring break, remember? It was cool connecting with things that are so ancient, and to think that they wound up preserved in rock and minerals. But I want to see other sites too. Besides, there's more to life than rocks, and I wanted to hang with you. And if it meant touching yucky zombified and dead things, that's what best friends do to be with each other."

"All those bones you dig for are dead," I pointed out.

"Yeah, but they've been dead for millions and millions of years," said Moondew, looking over her shoulder. "And we will be, too, if we don't get moving—Abby is moving pretty fast now!"

Luckily, we made it across the line before we collapsed. So happy that's over!

Honeybee queens are treated like babies, not royalty. Worker bees get to travel outside the hive, but queens stay inside, laying eggs. Workers eat honey made from nectar and "bee bread" made from pollen, but the only food a queen gets is royal jelly. It sounds fancy, but it is actually the baby food fed to all larvae in their first few days, and it's made from glands in the worker bees' heads!

Later, Moondew and I went to Nuts for Dough. I was glad that it's only four blocks from school—my legs were killing me! Despite all that pain, we still managed to get there before all the other kids from our school, and we got a table for once. Never underestimate the limping speed of a starving sixth grader in need of a donut fix.

My strategy to eat the cheapest things on the school menu this year had worked. It had left me with enough leftover lunch money to keep me in donuts over the summer.

I was so excited to see that Nuts for Dough had a

new donut! It has a honey-and-cream filling and is iced on top to look like a honeycomb. They call it the "Bee Good." And they *ARE* good—Moondew and I ate three. Well, maybe Moondew ate *two* and I mostly ate one plus a bite or two. When she likes something, she sure can pack it in. So, it's a good thing the donuts at Nuts for Dough aren't too expensive. We should suggest that Ms. Char buy those for our Science Squad meetings, instead of those nasty pre-boxed powdered things that she gets at the grocery store.

Then Moondew gave me a surprise she was going to save for the last day of school but decided I needed to have to celebrate the awesome donuts. She reached in her messenger bag (the one I sewed the silk ribbons to for her) and pulled out that ring with the little plastic bees floating in it. Far less tacky than it sounds, I swear. It's really cute! She found it at some flea market she went to with her mother, and she got one for herself, too, so now we are accessorized alike. With her being all into earthy casual, and me being into very preppy classic looks, I was surprised the ring went perfectly with both of our outfits. Some things can do that—be two seemingly different things at the same time.

We sat and ate our Bee Goods and slurped down unicorn iced teas and flashed our bee rings until we had to go home and do actual homework. I know, in the LAST WEEK OF SCHOOL! WHAT? SERIOUSLY?! Oh well, at least it'll be over soon.

It's gonna be a great summer!

Note to science self:

Honey is basically flower nectar mixed with bee spit. Bee spit tastes good. Who knew?

Note to fashion self:

Pay more attention to items that can be used across clothing styles. It seems like a good investment to only buy one accessory that goes with everything.

Catch Up: Last Week of School, Part 2

Eighth graders seem like a whole other species.

I like to watch them when I can. The way our middle school is arranged, they don't cross paths with us much. Their classes are on the other end of the school, with the seventh graders in the middle. But when I do see them, they seem so much bigger and mature and put together than the rest of us. Some of the best outfits come from a few eighth graders I've seen with interesting choices in clothing styles. They look like sleek, shiny wasps, while most of us in sixth grade look like larvae.

Seventh graders, on the other hand, seem to cross that divide. Some are short, some are gawky, some look old, some still look young, and some look just right. Like Shonda Fessler. She is arguably the prettiest seventh grader in our school, not to mention she has an amazing sense of personal style. Of course, she's popular. But not for why you think. It's because she's *nice* on top of it all. Like, the kind of person who says hi even when you are not the only two people in the hall.

She and I have advanced art together. There are only four of us in the class who aren't eighth graders, and we're two of them. So, we kind of stick together. In class, I mean. Which is nice, 'cause I get to look at whatever clothing choices she has made for the day, and I'm always impressed. Her style is so different from mine, but I think that developing a strong fashion eye has more to do with being open to a variety of different looks rather than just focusing on your own style. It doesn't mean I have to copy it, although a number of girls in seventh and sixth grade try to. But she's so eclectic that no one can guess how she will look. She does her own thing.

I want to be her. Sort of. I mean, I know I'll never be as tall as her, and I think I look stupid in braids, which she loves to experiment with, but I'd settle for being friends with her. Unfortunately, since I've been branded a science geek (not entirely sure when that started), it'll probably never happen.

We didn't talk much in class before this last quarter

when we sat at the same table in art. And that's how we got to talk one morning during the last week of school.

Before class started, I pulled out the flyer about the Science Squad National Convention. The best presentation of all the final badge projects from Science Squads in California gets to go represent our region at the national convention. And this year, it's in *Hawai'i!* I still haven't been to Hawai'i. The last squad that won from the Bay Area was in 1998, and they got to go to Springfield, Massachusetts. Which I am sure is nice. But it's not Hawai'i, so this chance shouldn't be wasted.

I was reading about the hotel when a voice said, "Oh, are you going to Hawai'i?"

It was Shonda, pointing to my brochure and leaning over to get a good look. My need to be seen as something more than a nerd took over, and I tried to cover the brochure from her stare.

"Uh," I very intelligently said. "Well, uh . . ."

"Oh!" she said, squinting her eyes to see the brochure better. "Are you in that Science Squad thing? My little brother is in that. He totally loves it. He said the older kids might get to go to Hawai'i. Is that you? Do you get to go?"

I sat there speechless, still in shock that she was talking to me. And not just *talking*, but actually trying to have a conversation. Like, it was more than just, "Excuse me, your elbow is in my paint palette," or, "Could you hand me one of those filbert-tip paintbrushes?" It was an actual conversation! Why did it have to be about my nerdy Science Squad! *ARGH!*

I finally managed to emit noise. "Yeah. Maybe. The Squad with the best presentation gets to go to the national convention, which is in Hawai'i . . . which is in the ocean." I stopped babbling.

"So you have to work over the whole summer on it? Wow, you must really love science," she said.

I winced. Ugh. *Always* a nerd.

"But I get it," she continued. "If you're really into something, it's worth it, right? Like I'm going to go to Junior Fashion Camp this summer—it's a ton of work, but it's so completely worth it if you are into fashion."

She tilted her head at me like she was just seeing me for the first time. "Come to think of it, do you like fashion? I remember those sketches you drew for that historical costume project we had, and you did that

22

perfect mishmash of eras. If you are into fashion, this would totally be your thing—you'd be great at it!"

She smiled, and I felt like the coolest sixth grader ever. Too bad only one other sixth grader saw it, and he couldn't have cared less because he always had his nose buried in his sketchbook.

And then the invisible cork came out of my mouth. "I *love* fashion," I said, telling her about my favorite designers and my attempts at sewing and about how I once got my anchor necklace stuck to some pink lace I was looking at at Britex and ended up having to buy an extra half yard of it because I couldn't get the necklace out.

She laughed. "Wow, Britex. I love that fabric store too. You really are into fashion. I had no idea! It's probably too late for summer, and you have your science thing, but they have a fall program that is like an after-school activity so you can fit it in with school. You should apply! It's cheaper than our after-school activities, and it's even free if you apply for and get one of the scholarships. Here, take this," she said, reaching into her bag and handing me a brochure and registration form for the camp. "This is a draft I was using to fill out my forms. But I finished them, and I don't need it anymore. You can just erase the marks I made and fill it in!"

This was my golden ticket, the way out of all nerd-dom and into being recognized as more than a future lab nut. Hello, fashion (and maybe even popularity if Shonda became my fashion buddy); goodbye, nerdy science rep. I couldn't possibly be nerdy anymore. There's no way someone could be both at the same time. They are two different things that can't exist on the same plane. And it looked like maybe fashion was going to win out for once.

I spent the rest of the day at school fantasizing about what a line of clothing would look like if Shonda and I designed it together. Oddly, everything I drew seemed to have something bee-themed in it. No fair, science! No infringing on my fashion time!

No more! That's it! I solemnly swear that I will NOT let science overshadow or take over my fashion stuff. No science allowed when I am working on fashion, and no fashion allowed when I am working on science. They just don't go together.

Catch Up:
LAST DAY of School!

You would think the last day of school would be super memorable, but it wasn't. I chalk this up to being a bit of—okay, a lot of—a nerd. The school thought that it was a great reward to give us free time outside, but the last thing I wanted to do was spend the day out in that horrible heat. Instead, Moondew and I helped Ms. Char clean out the science lab, where it was air-conditioned.

When I went out into the hall to dump a box of leftover handouts and unclaimed lab notes in the big recycle bin, I ran (literally) into Shonda. My lab notes and her fashion swatches and sketches flew all over the floor and mixed together.

I apologized as much as I could. I had a mouthful of donut because we'd convinced Ms. Char to let us bring them to the last class of the day. I bent down and started sifting through the material.

"Oh, it's okay. Don't worry about it. Really," said

Shonda as we sorted the paper and fabric. "I was helping clean up the art room, and it went pretty quick, so I got time to draw some stuff."

"These look really cool," I said, handing her the last of the sketches. "I like how you used the plaid on the side of this shirt."

"Yeah, I was practicing for camp. I'm a little nervous for it. Like, I can see clothes and outfits I want to put together, but designing the actual pieces feels really hard to me. You know that show, *Junior Designer Showdown?* How do they do it? I'm totally worried because camp is, like, twice the work of the fall program because they compact it. I also heard somewhere that they only offer admission once, and then you go to the bottom of the acceptance list. If you don't take it when they offer it, you may not get accepted for another two years! So, I can't chicken out and quit. I just gotta keep trying my best, I guess."

She blinked. Then she said, "Oh my gosh, wow, *sorry,* that was a lot. I didn't mean to just blurt like that. I just feel like I can talk to you. I don't know anyone who is really into fashion like we are. My friends are good at buying stuff and putting it together the way they see it online or on the mannequin at the store, but they never think outside of what someone else shows them."

Then she asked if I had applied.

I was completely stunned that she was confiding such secrets and opinions in me. I felt honored. And really surprised that she remembered encouraging me to apply for Fashion Camp. I said, "I did apply for fall but haven't heard yet."

"It always takes awhile," she said. "They have to go through all those applications and sketches and that giant wait-list. It's competitive, but I bet you'll get in. Don't worry, you have the whole summer before they will probably even reply."

We each went back to our hideaways. Once again, no one really saw me with the most popular seventh grader in our school.

I was still a science geek.

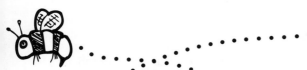

Catch Up:
First Week of Summer,
Wednesday, Part 1

The first week after school got out was a blur of hanging out at home, drawing and reading about bees. I should have caught up on journaling, but I was really loving not having homework, and sometimes journaling feels like work. I figure I'll be more consistent writing in this thing the rest of this summer, especially because I will have tons of time to do it. The bee project will only take a couple hours a day, so I should have plenty of time to journal.

You know how great it is when you have nothing to do, but you aren't bored? It was a whole week of that! I just waited for Science Squad activities to start and for that acceptance letter from Fashion Camp.

Mom finally started kicking me out of the apartment so she could get her work done. Apparently, my pacing

the hall was driving her crazy, and Barfley needed
walking anyway. A couple of times, Barfley and I met
~~Hannah~~ ~~Moondew~~ Sunshadow for our walks.

Total side note:

I'm not sure why Hannah chose Sunshadow as her
latest attempt to find her "natural name." Moondew
seemed perfectly natural, but she changed it. *Again.*
I'm gonna need to stop writing in ink. Or maybe I'll
just switch to calling her Hannah all the time. Who can
remember her new name when she changes it every
couple of weeks?

Anyway, I spent so much time waiting for the mail to
arrive that I almost forgot to feed Barfley! I'd find him
sitting on my bed with this sad look, peering out from
under his weirdly shaggy eyebrows. We still don't know
what breed he is (and we'll probably never know, since
he's a rescue dog), but he's big and furry, barely fits in
our apartment, and has the best expressions. I love all
of his doggie looks. Except for that one time when he
had that look that said, "I really love the taste of newly
purchased fabric. Thanks so much for leaving it out for

me!" But it's not his fault. I'm the one who keeps making him toys out of the leftover scraps from my projects.

And every day while Barfley crunched and slobbered through his massive bowl of stinky chow, I read and reread through the brochure that Shonda had given me. She was right; I could *totally* fit the fall program in after school, especially since I would be graduated from Science Squad by then.

Early Wednesday morning, I hiked up the hill and mailed the final forms for the summer Science Squad project in that evil mailbox. It did not try to bite me. Yet.

Then I spent a few hours hanging out with Hannah at Nuts for Dough and helping her decide which gemstones went best with her new summer skirts. We polished off a few Bee Goods and unicorn teas before she decided that it didn't really matter what colors went with her skirts since it was really about the "elemental source" she was feeling that day.

She should try pants sometime, because she tends to get down on the ground to look closer at rock and stone patterns she finds. I tried to convince her that pants might also be better for her to carry all of those pebbles and agates she collects and brings home. She said it's just easier to move in long skirts because they don't bind. I gave up.

We talked about bees for a while, and then I finally trudged home, my stomach full of sugar and my head full of ideas for fashions.

Everything would have been fine, except that later that day, I rifled through the mail my mom had set on the counter, and I *finally* received my letter from Junior Fashion Camp.

I screamed, and Mom came running out of her office/bedroom, probably thinking that something bad had happened. I think the last time I screamed that loud was when Barfley ate all my rainbow sour belts candy.

I tore open the envelope and skimmed the letter and registration information. I saw "accepted," "scholarship winner," "welcome," and "registration forms due by."

Which all meant that I got in. For *free!*

I didn't bother reading any more, but I jumped up and down with my mom, who was equally excited until she finally stopped jumping and asked me what we were so excited about.

I handed her the letter.

She smiled, and then it faded, and then she frowned. My heart sank.

"What is it?" I asked.

"Um, kiddo, I thought you applied for the fall program."

"I did!" I said.

"Well, this letter is offering you a spot in the summer camp."

WHAAAAT?!

Catch Up:
First Wednesday
of Summer, Part 2

Let's pause there for a moment.

Future me will definitely remember Six Flags
Amusement Park two summers back with the extended
family on Dad's side, when cousin Saritha and I ate too
much ice cream and cheese pizza and then went on the
Scream-er-ator.

Yeah, this moment was a lot like that. What came
next was just like the ups and downs on that roller
coaster. And how I felt pretty much matched how I felt
back then. Stomach churning, like I was going to be sick.

Step right up and ride the coaster of stress!
Admission is only one acceptance-letter-shaped ticket,
kids!

Welcome to Raksha's Big Mailbox Adventure!

Going Up: I got in to Fashion Camp! Woohoo!

Going Down: But it's for summer camp instead of fall! And I just mailed my final forms for the Science Squad final project a few hours ago! I am already committed there! *ARGH!* (Everybody scream!)

Up: (From Mom) "You worked so hard this year, I want you to have a relaxing summer. So, you should only do one thing. Just apply again but for fall, like you meant to."

Down: (Throw your hands in the air and scream

like you mean it!) I hear Shonda's words in my head: "They only offer admission once, and then you go to the bottom of the acceptance list if you don't take it, and you may not get accepted for another two years."

Up: *But I just put that last set of forms in the mail for Science Squad for the summer bee project! Maybe I can get it back out and change the forms to request doing my project in the fall. That will work out better. I won't have to meet with Mari anymore, and summer Fashion Camp will give me a leg up on starting seventh grade with a notch in my popularity belt for sure. And I pretty much can't say no to Fashion Camp now, or I'll NEVER get in.*

Okay! Time to go get the letter back from the mailbox!

Down: *My hand is stuck in that STUPID mailbox! What am I going to do? Fashion or science, fashion or science?*

Up: *Yay! The mailman!*

Down: *He's laughing at me.*

Up: *Yay! He got me out! (Again.)*

Down: *But without the Science Squad forms.*

What a great ride, right kiddies?! Bathrooms are on the left. Have a nice day, and we hope you enjoyed your ride on Raksha's Big Mailbox Adventure!

Catch Up:
First Wednesday
of Summer, Part 3

So that's it.

I thought for sure that this offer for summer camp was a mistake on their end, but I figured I should verify what box I had checked before I called and freaked out all over the Fashion Camp people. Every scientist and fashion designer knows that when you are measuring, you should measure two or three times to double- and triple-check that your answers and data are accurate.

I looked and found my copies of the registration form for the camp, and there it was on the form—a check in the box that said "summer camp"!

Only I hadn't put it there.

It was there from when Shonda had used that same form as practice for her registration. I had forgotten to change it when I had used it as my actual registration form. I thought I'd erased everything. Oops.

My forms were on their way, confirming my registration for the Science Squad summer project, which wasn't a bad thing. I really wanted to do it.

At least I'm back inside, instead of being stuck in the rain, and I've caught up on my journal. I am sitting here on my bed with my head propped up on Barfley, who smells like wet dog. Why does he smell? He spends all day in the apartment!

I'd like to say I am thinking (that's what I told Mom I'm doing), but really, I spent a little amount of time sniffling. Maybe bawling. I'm not sure why. My science brain knows that nothing other than my pride was hurt this afternoon at the mailbox. Rain can't hurt me, and I'm still getting to help real scientists this summer.

And that's the thing. I don't know what I was thinking. This is not a big deal. People really only become one thing in life, right? And maybe this is my one thing for now.

And I totally forgot that the bee stuff only can be done in the summer because that's the best time to catch ZomBees.

Not to mention the final badge assessment for the project competition at the national convention is done after this summer for the next convention. The *Hawaiʻi* convention. Who knows when the national convention will be there again? If I did my final project in the fall, I'd have to wait until the end of next summer for the assessment to go to the national convention, and I'd be in a squad with a bunch of people I didn't spend the last four years with, including Hannah-Moondew-Sunshadow.

Yep, it's better this way. I've been waiting four years to get that last badge.

Except that I really really REALLY want to start seventh grade with some social credibility, and Fashion Camp would totally be my way in. I can imagine talking with Shonda in advanced art about our fashion ideas. When people see me in the halls, instead of saying, "Hey, there goes that smart girl who won the science fair last year," or worse, "Who's that?" (or the absolute worst, not even noticing me), they'd say, "That's Shonda's fashion friend!" There wouldn't be a speck of science mentioned in the sentence.

SUMMER TO-DO LIST:

2. Handwash the silk pillow that is just like me—half
   Indian, half Chinese. The sari fabric side smells like
   Barfley 'cause he had his butt on it while I was using
   him as a headrest. When I outgrew my last Chinese
   New Year jammies and finally made the "me" pillow,
   I didn't intend for it to be a dog bed! Barfley, if
   you can read, THIS IS NOT A CUSHION FOR YOUR
   FURRY RUMP!

Note to both selves:

   Be very careful about seemingly small details, and
double-check every form before you send it in.

The best time to hunt ZomBees is in spring and
summer, when honeybees (like most humans) are most
active. Many types of bees go into hibernation when fall
arrives. While honeybees do not hibernate, they do retreat
into their hives. They work hard to gather and make food in
the warmer months so they have supplies to eat while they
cluster together in winter to share body heat.

Second Monday
of Summer

So today we had the first Science Squad meeting at the library for our new summer project. We're at the end of the blue level and just have to finish our last badge project. I'm really glad we are almost done because it'll mean no more Mari, but I will miss the work I get to do with Science Squad. When it's over, I'll just have to find other ways to scratch my science itch.

Ms. Char put out the donuts. Those chalky, powdered, raspberry-filled rings are just weird. How do they get the jelly into the ring? It's just not right. She verified that we all had our forms in, which, it turns out, we could have brought to the meeting today (somewhere, the evil mailbox is laughing, LAUGHING I tell you!). Then she talked to us about ZomBee Trackers—the research project we'd be helping—and ways to get started, and teamwork. Then, for the first time ever, she sat down in the corner and told us to go for it.

It's a little frightening but also exhilarating to have complete control over our destinies. Or maybe I should say *Mari* has complete control.

Because sure enough, the second Ms. Char sat down in the corner, Mari stood up and said, "I'd like to volunteer to be the leader for our efforts on this project. All in favor?" She held up her own hand and nodded enthusiastically at us, her wavy brown hair bouncing on her shoulders.

The donuts were already out, so I would have lost my bet that she'd do it before the donuts were put out. But seriously, couldn't she wait?! And it's a good thing the library is a fairly noisy one and we always have the same meeting room with a solid door, because Mari's voice is really loud. Especially when she's trying to be the ~~alpha dog~~ queen bee.

No one reacted.

Okay, I ~~may have~~ snorted. It's not *my* fault—Quiet Kenny fluffed his napkin, which had powdered donut stuff on it, and a bit of it flew into my nose. I made a big show of blowing my nose to prove it when Mari scowled at me and pushed her headband back.

~~Hannah~~ Sunshadow kept writing her name over and

over again in her journal, varying the thickness and swirl count on each vowel, and didn't bother looking up. The twins, Jayden and Keyarie, were (as usual) arguing over who had more donuts, so they probably didn't hear Mari. Quiet Kenny was sitting with his head tilted toward the ceiling, slowly eating his donut. I looked up, too, but there was nothing there except for the lights, one of which was buzzing.

Mari frowned and dropped her hand. "Did you guys hear me? I'm volunteering to do the hardest part!" Her voice got louder (if that was possible) as she rapped on the table with her knuckles. I heard Ms. Char rustle in her seat. All of us but Sunshadow finally looked at Mari.

"Maybe we should figure out what the parts are first, before we decide which is most important," said Sunshadow, still looking at her journal. Now she was adding bees and rocks around her name.

Mari paused for a moment, apparently calculating. Then she said, "That's a good idea. I'll guide the discussion."

After that, we described what we wanted to do for the bees and all the tasks we thought we'd have to do to get that done. I thought we did a pretty good job. We decided to call ourselves the ZomBee Hunters Guild, and we came up with a big list of things to do.

"So, we've decided that in addition to the data collection, we are going to try and find some way to bring awareness to the problem. Oh, and do some fundraising and donate money to the research project," Mari said, summarizing our efforts. Ms. Char excused herself for a moment, so we were alone as a group.

We broke into pairs: me and Sunshadow, Kenny and Jayden, and Mari and Keyarie. But when we divided stuff up, Mari was not going to be collecting the bees or handling them if they needed to be mailed in to the researchers. She would just be entering the data into the database for the group as we collected it.

I was pretty sure that building the light traps to attract zombie bees and collecting the specimens would really be the hardest parts, mostly because those things would take time.

The lights are pretty straightforward. You take a compact fluorescent light bulb in one of those bulb cages and turn it upside down over a funnel in a bucket or some other sort of container to catch any bees. All you have to do is attach it to the container so it doesn't fall over. And you can use all sorts of different containers and funnels.

Like this:

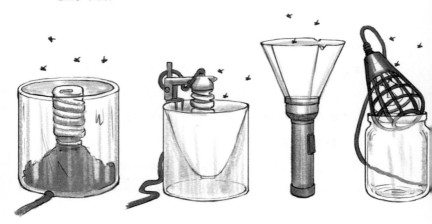

Finding a bee near a light does not mean the bee is a ZomBee. Sometimes, regular worker bees can be stuck outside the hive at night. And just like ZomBees, they can be attracted to lights. There is no sure way to tell if your dead or dying bee is infected unless you see larvae hatch from the bee or unless pupae are found with it.

But then we have to search for dead bees, figure out if we can put lights wherever we find them (we have to ask permission if they're on private property), build the lights, install them, check them regularly for any specimens, collect the specimens, record the number of bees, and watch the collected specimens for signs of infection (ew). Then the specimens have to be recorded in the database and mailed in—if the scientists request them.

That's a lot of tasks for one team. So I said so.

Mari glared at me, then said, "Afraid of a little work, Raksha? How *exactly* did you beat me last year in the All-Star Science Show?"

"It's not that I'm afraid to work. It's just a lot, and I'm not the only one who thinks so." Everyone else nodded. "Look at how much time it will take to do all that, and we have to figure out a way to bring awareness to the problem *and* raise money?"

I could see the wheels turning in her head.

"Fine, let's redistribute the tasks," said Mari. "Keyarie and I will build the light traps, and the rest of you can search, install, and collect, and then Keyarie and I will record our findings in the database as we go. We will all work on thinking up ideas of where we can put the traps and on how to bring awareness to the issue."

Everyone seemed to think that was okay, but I noticed that she still wouldn't be handling specimens.

Of course, Ms. Char returned at this moment when everything was fine.

I was a little mad. Okay, a *LOT* mad at Mari. We've been competing over the years for things, and sometimes I win, and sometimes she does. But I always work hard. She is a total jerk for saying that I don't. She just said that because she's still mad she came in second. Her problem is that she only sees one thing. She can't be a treasurer or a secretary because to her, there is only president and not-president. Winner and not-winner.

Ms. Char beamed at us and told us how awesome we were and patted Mari on the back for handling the discussion. (Insert eye roll here). When she showed us the website where we would be logging in our results, and keeping our shared folders for the project, I started getting hot around my neck.

Good thing we had a break.

Hannah and I retreated outside the room into the music area of the library.

"Typical Mari," said Hannah.

"Yeah, she always has to get her way. Let's talk about something other than her."

"Like what?"

I told Hannah about the Fashion Camp problem, and you know what she said?

"Do both."

"Whaaaat?"

"Seriously, you should do both. Like, there's no reason not to now that we've sort of balanced the tasks. Besides, it's already paid for because you got the scholarship."

"My mom said to do just one thing this summer." I know I sounded whiny, but I couldn't help it.

"I know you aren't the most rebellious human on Earth, but it's not like she said you couldn't go to camp. She just wanted you to have fun this summer, and for you, fashion is fun. It may give me a headache, but for you, it's somehow really exciting. I think the universe is trying to tell you something, and you should pay attention.

"I know you think that it might bring you some sort

of popularity, and maybe it will. Although I don't know why you worry about that anyway. But if it makes you happy, you should go for it."

I looked at my calendar and thought about the registration letter for Fashion Camp. I could totally fit it in. I could do Squad meetings, scouting locations, and setting and collecting traps on Monday, Wednesday, and Friday mornings, and then Fashion Camp in the afternoons, leaving Tuesdays and Thursdays for more trap-checking and fashion work. The studio workroom for Fashion Camp is just five blocks from the library. Mom and Dad don't know how long it will take to do the bee project. If I am gone all day, they won't notice any difference, and I'm always sewing something, so that wouldn't be any different. I mean, as it is, I get myself up, fed, and on the bus in the mornings for school.

I started to get excited, my anger with Mari turning into a thrill of anticipation for Fashion Camp. Maybe I could do this.

"But it has to be secret. I don't want my parents to think I am too stressed or overscheduled," I said.

Then I had a thought.

"I don't know if I can be fashion *and* science girl this

summer. They're just so different. I kind of have to be in the right frame of mind for each one."

"I don't get why you can't be two things at the same time."

"Yeah, right, at the same time—that'd be great. You just can't be two totally different things at once. I'll end up getting confused and making fashions for bees, like this."

I drew these lovely latest and greatest fashions for bees:

We went back in the room after our break, talking about how we could do our bee collection. Only Mari was back.

"Glad to see you are on track," said Mari. "We really need everyone on board for this and working at full capacity if we're going to go to Hawai'i . . . I mean, the national convention."

"Yeah, it would be cool to go to Hawai'i," I admitted. "And I am totally on track for a very productive and fun summer."

"And don't worry," said Hannah, "we'll be putting in plenty of hours, and Fashion Camp totally won't interfere."

I would have smacked my forehead, but it would have been too obvious. What part of "secret" did Hannah not get?

"Wait, *what*?" said Mari. "Who's at Fashion Camp? You guys can't be doing anything else! We need to be totally committed 110 percent to Science Squad—we're almost there, you guys! Almost done!" Her voice bordered on hysterical. "Nothing can get in the way of my, um, *our* trip to Hawai'i, our last badge, and the end of blue level.

There's no Fashion Camp, not on my watch. I can't do everything, and neither can you!"

I had a slight twinge in my stomach. A feeling like maybe she was right.

Then I thought of how she'd managed to avoid touching the bees and samples, leaving us to do all the work, and how self-centered she was. And she'd tried to call me lazy when she was trying to avoid work. No way was I giving in on this.

"Lighten up," I said. "It'll be at a different time, and I will still do all my Science Squad duties."

"Do your parents know about this?" said Mari, trying another tactic. She always assumes that everyone has achievement-obsessed parents like hers.

"They know," I lied. "And what I do is none of your *beeswax* anyway."

And then I knew how to really throw her off the trail.

"I'm totally great at science—that's why I won the last science competition, *remember?*" I gave her a wide, toothy grin and stuck my chin out.

She scowled and walked away.

I'm so doing this.

Second Wednesday
of Summer

The hardest part about hunting ZomBees in San Francisco is trying to decide what to wear. Layering is best, which is easy if you wear fairly classic looks. This morning, I put on flats, black capri pants (yes, *pants*—it's still true that no self-respecting San Franciscan wears shorts, even in summer), and a polo shirt under a hoodie. You really can't wear skirts here (despite Hannah's best efforts). It's just too cold, and we get hit with strong winds and afternoon breezes rolling off of the Pacific all year round.

This all got me wondering how the bees manage to be so active here in San Francisco. If they let their flight muscles get chilled, they can't fly as well, so how do they manage in the rain, breezes, and fog? I read somewhere that honeybees can fly at a constant speed even *against* headwinds, so I guess nature just finds a way.

Mom came out of her bedroom/office to give me a kiss goodbye as I left to meet Hannah to scout locations for our traps. She must not have any meetings today, because she was wearing plaid jammie pants and her favorite T-shirt with Donald Duck holding a golf club and the words "Ready for the Weekend." Even if she had a meeting, she'd be "sporting" (her word, not mine) San Francisco tech casual, like yoga pants and fleece tops over some sort of T-shirt. That's better than Dad, I guess, who pretty much always wears a button-down shirt, jeans, and (shudder) *white tennis shoes.*

I don't know where I get my interest in fashion from, because it sure isn't from them. I really do care about clothes, even though some people might look at my wardrobe and conclude I'm a tiny, uptight golfer. I just dress this way because it's easier and my parents don't really budget much for clothes. It's not unusual for designers to have a personal style that is totally different from the fashions they create, so maybe that'll be me. The outfits in my head and my sketchbook look very little like what I wear, anyway. Maybe I'll become one of those designers who always wear the same basic things, like Vera Wang or Carolina Herrera.

When I reached the top of the hill, I mailed in the registration confirmation from Fashion Camp. The mailbox didn't try to eat me this time, thank goodness.

The rest of the way, I kept thinking about Fashion Camp. It's not really rebelling if your parents want you to go, just not yet, but you are actually willing to do the work now rather than later, right? Mom and Dad work really long hours, and I don't want to have to pester them all the time to be taken somewhere or picked up, so this will be less effort for them. Win–win!

Second Wednesday of Summer (later)

Hannah and I met at Nuts for Dough. And as usual, she was dressed like a blind hippie! I had tried to help her with her fashion problem again just last month. After all, Hannah is totally mellow about trying on my weird creations, so I figured I owed her some fashion help in return. She still looks good in anything, but since she insists on being bohemian, I just worked with what she has. I showed her how to combine her crazy closet of mishmashed colors and textures. But once again, she forgot it all. I think she just grabs whatever is in front of each rod, stack, or drawer.

Anyway, Hannah wore a long skirt and a tie-dye top under an army jacket. *Bleh.* At least she remembered to swap the granny boots for tennis shoes, since we had a long way to walk. I guess it doesn't really matter—I'm not sure the fashion gods care what you wear when you're ZomBee hunting, as long as it's practical.

We walked ~~five miles~~ a really long way, looking under lights for dead bees, and we found some! In just an hour, we had three places marked on our maps to bring to the next Science Squad meeting, where we'll decide which spots get light traps. I was excited because finding those places quickly meant we got to figure out my route to Fashion Camp from the library even sooner.

Hannah and I found the perfect way to go in between my activities. No local really sets foot on the cable cars, but one line goes right by the library, and I can get off a block from the workroom for the Fashion Camp. We tried it, and it was super easy!

When we stopped at the library, I uploaded the schedule we could use for collecting our specimens to the shared file folders. Then we parted ways, and I went home to practice for camp by sketching some ideas for fashions.

My pencil lead kept breaking. So annoying! But if this is the worst I have to deal with, that's okay by me.

Who knew juggling two lives could be this easy?

First Day of Fashion Camp!

I can't believe how exciting Fashion Camp was today! Shonda was totally surprised to see me and gave me a huge hug. And we sat together the whole time. And she didn't talk to anyone else. Okay, maybe she did, but I didn't notice because she mostly talked to me.

When she asked me what happened to Science Squad, I told her I was doing both, and she looked at me like I'd grown antennae and wings!

"This camp is going to be a ton of work!" she said. "A friend of my mom's said her son did it two years ago, and he was busy all day." Then she thought for a moment. "But everybody's different, right? You're smart. I bet you can do both. I'm just so glad you came for summer! This is gonna be like old times in art class—so fun!"

She said "old times" like we had been friends forever!

I felt my nerdy side melt away like honey stirred into hot tea. *YAAAY!* I love my fashion friend!

And I love the workroom too! It's a bright loft on the third floor of a really pretty art deco building a few blocks from Union Square. It has five huge floor-to-ceiling windows on the street side and a bunch of black worktables and stools, just like *Junior Designer Showdown*. There are dress forms by each stool, and we each got a glossy black notebook for our handouts and our plans for designs. I can't wait to fill that thing with notes, ideas, and sketches.

The main instructor is Lydia Pence, and she's really cool. She was wearing a long, flowing chiffon skirt, a fitted black T-shirt, a cropped leather jacket, and biker boots. (A skirt! Made of lightweight materials! In San Francisco! Maybe Hannah is on to something . . .) On anyone else, this would have looked absurd. But it worked on her. She also had these really cool thick black eyeglasses, the kind the eighth-grade math teacher at my school wears, but on Lydia, they look totally acceptable. Huh.

Anyway, she announced that we would each be creating a three-piece collection, and each of us would also create and set up our own mini runway show to present the fashions! We'll pick our own place to show, even if it's just home or the workroom. And we'll send invitations to everyone in the room, so we will all see one another's collections.

Wow, this is going to be a lot of work, but I can't wait!

I am ECSTATIC!

We got to check out the supply room, where they had a few remnants—piles of trim and some other stuff—that we can use for our project. But Lydia said we have to provide our own fabric. Luckily, I still have a sewing project fund from the money I earned last summer working for Grandpa Chen filing paperwork at his real estate office. It doesn't go that far if I am buying expensive fabrics, but most of my purchases are from the remnant bins and "yard sale" at Britex anyway.

Once again, I daydreamed about me and Shonda doing fashion things together. Maybe we could even sit together at school sometimes. Hannah wouldn't mind hanging out with her. She said Shonda has an old, kind soul, like one of the world's largest rocks, Uluru.

The ride home on the cable car was awesome. I love

playing "Who's a Tourist?" Today, it was pretty much everyone sitting near me. As we came over the hilltop, I tried to look at the city through their eyes. The late afternoon sun reflected on the buildings, making it look like a city of gold. Like a city full of possibilities. I wanted to yell, "It's *TRUE!* Anything is possible here! Look at me! I am a scientist AND a designer!" But I didn't. I just finished the ride and got off, practically skipping the rest of the way home.

Well, I skipped *almost* all of the way home. I stopped and stuck my tongue out at the evil mailbox as I went past it. But I stayed about three feet from it, just in case it was hungry.

Today was so great!

I Don't Remember What Day of Summer Today Is

Today was a nightmare!

I'm sorry I keep forgetting to journal! My arms and neck are really stiff. Carrying two bags all day is a pain in the neck! My neck has as crick in it, probably because I wear both the backpack and the messenger bag at the same time, but it's the only way to carry all the stuff I need for both of my lives. And of course, today that heat wave came back, so I was huffing and puffing and sweating by the time I got to the library, and I'm pretty sure I smelled . . . not so good.

Which would be no big deal if it weren't for the fact that I always seem to end up next to Quiet Kenny at the meetings. And I didn't want him to think I smell. I have discovered that somewhere along the way, he became kind of cute. He's also kind of nice, even if he does not say much and always seems to be off in space.

When I sat down today with all my luggage, he was

63

watching the back of the squeaky meeting-room door, so he didn't react to me sitting down, which is probably good. I think. I mean, it's better than him snorting a big noseful of Raksha sweat and then running for the door, gagging, right?

When we handed out supplies, Mari mentioned that her hardware store was out of bulb cages. She said they would be getting some over the weekend. But she still has more lights to make, so we rescheduled Monday's meeting to Tuesday afternoon.

Which is the time I had set aside for Fashion Camp fabric shopping at Britex.

Then she babbled some more about how we all have to be committed to this one last project, since we are all working together and have to rely on one another, and that nothing can get in the way of us finishing strong. Blah, blah, blah. Whatever.

Then she smiled at me like the Cheshire cat, and I don't know why.

So I just smiled back and went with it. It just means I have to work on my designs that night and ask Mom if she'll take me to Britex some other time between now and the next Fashion Camp session.

After the Science Squad meeting, I had to go to Fashion Camp. I got all sweaty again, not only from the walk but also from the added stress of trying to figure out how to rearrange my schedule. I was worried that Shonda would think I was gross, but it was completely fine. We sit far enough apart at the worktable that I don't think she even noticed.

As I set my backpack down, a broken bulb cage I'd replaced yesterday fell out onto the floor. I didn't know my backpack was unzipped.

"What's that?" asked Shonda.

"It's a part of my science stuff," I said, inspecting the zipper. It was broken—probably an easy fix. I explained how we use the cages to make light traps.

"Oh," she said. "I thought it was part of your stuff for your designs! I was thinking that it was very experimental, like maybe you were having an Alexander McQueen moment. I'm such an idiot."

I laughed as I stuffed the cage back into the backpack. "No, you aren't. I mean, if I'm gonna spill something here, it should be fashion stuff, right?"

And we got back to learning. Today, we learned about ways to finish hems, but all I could do was think about the bee lights and how many I had to check every day.

Argh. I hope this doesn't happen again.

SUMMER TO-DO LIST:

29. Fix zipper on backpack.

Some Day in the
Middle of Summer

Of course, it happened again. Sorry I haven't kept up, but it has been totally busy. I think I'm not going to bother trying to catch up anymore.

I feel like I'm stuck on fast-forward. I have so much to do, even though I get up early and go to bed late. Maybe Mom was right, and I needed a relaxing summer. But honestly, everything would be fine if the Science Squad stuff was just consistent.

We have rescheduled and even added a couple of Science Squad meetings from my original schedule! I have been waiting for it to get better, but it's only getting worse! This time, we rescheduled our meetings for the next few Tuesdays. Keyarie had a dance thing that came up, and where she goes, Jayden has to go. She looked really uncomfortable when she told us and kept looking at me. Did I look that sleep deprived? It's not *her* fault. The looks Jayden was giving her, you know he's mad (those two still don't get along). But if one-third of the Squad can't make it, then something needs to change.

This means that I barely have time to check light traps with Hannah, go to Fashion Camp, and then do my fashion work, which is what I normally do on Tuesday and Thursday. Guess I'll just stay up later to get stuff done. Since it's summer, Mom and Dad don't mind. As far as they know, I'm just having a *relaxing* break, not trying to be two people at the same time.

Everything is getting harder to juggle. It's like the schedule is OUT TO GET ME. In favor of science and not fashion—'cause that's the time that keeps being eaten up.

And speaking of eaten up, one of Hannah's bee samples suddenly has little brown pupae in the bag. So sad! And *gross* and . . . exciting! I'm disappointed it didn't happen to a bee in my half of our collected specimens, but we agreed to take turns bringing our collected bees home so that we can both do monitoring and reporting. After we report this one, a red marker will show on the map where we collected it, and we can show everyone "our" mark on the ZomBee Trackers website. I probably shouldn't be so excited that one of our bees was infected and died. What a way to go! No one wants to die with a maggot pushing out between their head and thorax. But it really was cool . . .

Samples in my collection: 5

Samples showing infection: 0 (Lucky Hannah!)

Another Midsummer Day

I love Britex! I'm so glad I finally found time to shop here. I just wish they were open later and were closer to my house. Mom brought me there today, but then her cell rang with an office emergency, so she went outside to take the call. I don't usually spend much time anywhere other than the fourth floor, so I told her I'd stay there.

I started sifting through yard-sale fabrics and remnants, looking for hidden goodies like a bee gathering pollen. It took half an hour, but I found some beautiful ombré silk that shifted from cream on top to a slate blue on the bottom. I could make it into my final dress! I was lucky because silk usually doesn't last once it's in this area. Not only did I find silk but I found it in the yard-sale fabrics—and for an additional discount on top of that!

Once Mom was back, I went to the third floor and stared at all of the trims and embellishments.

My head swam—but not with possibilities. It was just *overwhelming*. There were so many things, and yet nothing looked right for my designs. Actual lace? Nope. Fringe? Nope. Buttons, silk cord, feathers, bric-a-brac? Nope, nope, nope, and nope. I even considered leather flowers and pearls. Nope.

I forgot that design takes time. It's not like my science stuff, where I just try the same thing over and over with a change in variable and then record the results. I'm trying to create something out of my head that doesn't exist yet. It's exhausting. Now I have to stay up late tonight again to work on my notes about the bee samples.

Samples in my collection: 9

Samples showing infection: 0

Fourth Whatever Day
It Is of . . . Whatever

Today I fell asleep on the cable car and had to walk three blocks uphill to get back to the stop I wanted. Ugh. And I had to do it with both the backpack and the messenger bag. At least it wasn't too hot.

One good thing happened today. Kenny just started talking to me for no reason, asking me about our bee samples and if we got any more infected bees. I said no, but did he have any? And he said no, and that he's been sampling all sorts of places, and he's pulled in tons of other samples. Anyway, I wondered what other samples he meant, but I couldn't figure out how to ask without sounding like an idiot. Because it's possible that I missed a part of our assignment, since I am so tired lately.

But he seemed interested in talking to me. And he said more than one or two things. What does it mean? He also offered me half of his donut 'cause he said he noticed I seem to really like them and he'd had a huge lunch. I said thanks and took it and nibbled at it.

Shonda asked me if I was okay today, since I was sitting facedown at our worktables this afternoon. I couldn't help it; I only meant to rest my head. I asked if I could copy her notes from the lecture I had missed, and she said yes. I'm lucky to have her as a friend.

Yet Another Midsummer Day

Today the Science Squad schedule changed again. We're barely a month into summer, and I don't even know what day it is half the time. Things are getting *RIDICULOUS.* We have more Science Squad meetings on Tuesdays and Thursdays for reasons that I don't even remember, but we all show up anyway. I end up having to cut my design time or donut time with Hannah.

A Day in . . . Summer

Argh! Today, we had another Thursday meeting, and that meant another whole week of daily Science Squad meetings and almost no time to work on fashion design stuff in the workroom lab time. I don't know how I am going to get anything done when the schedule keeps changing. I don't know what day to be where or when. I completely slept through my alarm this morning. My mom noticed I was still in bed and woke me up two hours after I was supposed to be awake! Hannah is usually mellow, but she looked a little cranky when I caught up with her two blocks from Nuts for Dough. I made it up to her with an extra Bee Good.

It's Daytime . . . I Think

I just realized I forgot to send in data to Mari for two days because I was trying to make up the time for design work. It's hard to do at night at home, though, because I don't have a great workspace, and the workroom is closed at night. I'm too tired to write. I'll catch up later.

Day Something-or-Other

I completely forgot I was going to bring in my fashion books for Shonda to borrow today. I'm worried for her. She seems really frustrated with her designs, and I was thinking the books might give her inspiration. I felt so bad when I got to Fashion Camp today. She looked so hopeful when I came in, and I could practically taste her disappointment when I told her I forgot the books.

"It's okay," she said. "I really am starting to think that maybe I just don't have what it takes."

"That is totally not true!" I said. "Look, if you just tweak this sleeve, you have something different and fresh. May I?"

She nodded, and I lightly sketched on her idea.

"Oh, *wow*, I just love it!" she said. "I wouldn't have thought to do that. You totally have that eye. I can add accessories to show off that change. Thanks!" And she *hugged me. At least one thing is going right.*

Samples in my collection: 15

Samples showing infection: 0

Wrong Day

Oops, I showed up at Fashion Camp on the wrong day. ARGH! Enough said.

The Day of the Donuts

I may have gotten myself barred from Nuts for Dough FOREVER.

Yesterday, we had another schedule switch, and I ended up staying up late again to finish my sketches and some sewing. This morning when collecting bee samples, I kept yawning and worrying with every yawn that I might suck in a bee. Luckily, it was sort of foggy and cold, so there wasn't as much bee activity, just lots of motionless bee specimens. If they weren't dead, they were pretty sluggish.

It was Hannah's turn to take the samples home for monitoring, but she couldn't because she had to go straight from our donut time to her grandma's birthday party. So I put them in my backpack with my bee stuff.

We went to Nuts for Dough for our Bee Goods, and I almost fell asleep in my unicorn tea. I thought caffeine was supposed to help keep you awake. Nope. Totally didn't work for me.

Hannah's mom came and got her, so I was on my own and tired and distracted. When I got up to go catch the cable car down to Fashion Camp, I grabbed my messenger bag and totally forgot to grab the backpack.

The backpack that was full of bee samples in zippered baggies, by the way.

Some of which were *not fully closed.*

And some of those bees were still capable of flight. Even in their confused, possibly zombified state, they could still get out of the gap in the not-yet-fixed zipper and fly around.

Oops.

It's a well-known fact that bees not only make honey but they also eat honey themselves. Of course, that's why they make it. And *these* bees smelled those honey-filled donuts. Lots of them. Trays of them.

I'm glad I wasn't there to witness the bees getting cozy in the warmth of the shop and their flight muscles heating up. I also missed them flying out of my backpack to see the bright lights and find the source of all that honey. And I missed the part where people actually ran out of the store. I hope that none of the bees were just normal confused workers, because if they manage to get back to the hive, they can tell their sisters all about this great place where they can get tons of honey. Bees have been known to rob each other's honey stash from hive to hive in full-on bee wars. And an army of bees with theft on their minds is not something you want to see in a donut shop. EVER.

Hannah's the one who saw the "Closed" sign in the window on her way home from the party and checked the Nuts for Dough social feed to see what was up. After she told me about it, I checked for photos, but there weren't any. But I imagine the actual scene at the donut shop today looked like this:

Oh yeah, and the backpack has my name and phone number on it.

Oops.

Day of Meh

Pink is not the only color known to all girl-kind in fashion. Why does everyone insist that everything for girls be pink? Don't get me wrong, I like pink, just not on everything.

I swear half the designs other girls in Fashion Camp are making are pink dresses. Like they are fashion-industry clones or robots or something. Or worker bees.

Shonda is different, just like me. She's avoiding pink too. It really is nice to have a friend who gets that you want to try something different than what the stores tell you to wear.

We made mood boards today. The idea is you gather a bunch of stuff like pictures, magazine clippings, and fabric bits. You can even add random things you find interesting, like candy wrappers or pretty labels from pop bottles or bits of quotes and text. And you put all this stuff in one place, and that is your mood board! It's meant to show the mood of the collection you are designing and keep you on track and inspired. Mine had some quotes about Audrey Hepburn, a Bee Good donut bag with this pretty honey-colored text on it, pictures of 1940s dresses, and a cluster of silk flower hairpins Grandma Su gave me. I want to design classic women's fashions. Girly without being covered in ruffles and overly romantic, and absolutely, for sure, positively NO PINK. That's just too obvious.

Shonda's board is mostly pictures of clothes and accessories that already exist. I think some of them are even from her own closet. That's a good idea if you design for yourself, but I'm not going that route.

My own designs are coming along okay, I guess. They are classic but kind of meh, and I just don't know if I have time to fix them. The last piece, my fancy dress, is the worst. It's missing something. It looks nice, but it's just really basic. Something needs to be changed, but no amount of trim or piping or any of my other "borrowed from Chanel" tricks are working. All my designs look half-done, but I'm not falling into that giant pink vortex of glitter, gloss, and sequins.

'Cause I have ZomBees to hunt and dead things to collect.

Nuts for Dough called, so Dad got my backpack on the way home from work yesterday. He didn't say anything to me about what they said, so I figured it was a good idea not to ask. He didn't even look mad. He just told me not to forget my stuff all over the city. Then he ruffled my hair, and we all had some nice hot vada that he brought home from the Indian restaurant next door to Nuts for Dough for an appetizer. He said all those sugary donuts put him in the mood for a delicious savory ring of dough.

Vada are delicious, but Bee Goods they are not.

I don't think I'll ever eat a Bee Good again. Unless I ask Hannah or my mom to smuggle some home for me. And I am not above begging. So maybe I will eat another, but I will never go back there again. I can't. It's too mortifying.

Day of the Dog, Samples on the Shelf, and Things in the Compost Bin

Every dog has a favorite food, and Barfley's is peanut butter. So it wasn't his fault, not really . . .

Did I remember to mention that I have to keep my bee samples out on the flowerpot shelf outside our kitchen window?

And that wouldn't be a big deal if silk wasn't fairly slippery. I'll get to that part in a sec.

Mom and Dad are cool with the science, but they have a thing about the idea of tiny fly larvae exploding out of other insects in our already-too-small apartment. And since I have to wait a week for signs of infection to appear so I can record them, the samples have to sit around for a long time. It's not like we have a garage or somewhere else to keep them. And it's probably a good idea to keep the samples out of Barfley's reach.

So I carefully open the kitchen window and put the sample containers into a small plastic storage box that sits on the ledge outside and wait. And wait. None of the bees in my samples have burst open, and I haven't seen any pupae . . . yet. Out of all our samples, only that one bee Hannah took home had the pupae in a few days. Ew. We had to send that sample to the university for examination.

Anyway, one of the big problems I have lately is that when I'm tired, I not only become forgetful, I get clumsy. Like, I trip over my own feet. It doesn't help that I'm going through a growth spurt.

So today, I carefully opened the window (and left it open 'cause it was hot), put the samples in the box, and then set the box onto the flowerpot ledge. Don't worry, nothing happened to them. All of my samples are dead (or at least not moving), so there's no risk of them flying away like some did in the donut shop.

I could really use a Bee Good right now. Dang it.

Anyway, this evening after dinner, I worked on the silk that I got at Britex for one of my uninspired fashions. It just needed something more, so I thought I'd use lace and an airbrush to create a little more texture on the piece. But I wanted to be very exact about where I put the pattern, so I wanted to cut the pieces out first.

There's no room on my bedroom floor anymore. It's covered with fabric scraps and crumpled pieces of sketchbook paper and even some colored-pencil shavings. Definitely not a safe place for the delicate texture of silk, nor is it a good place to spread something out flat.

In fact, I discovered there aren't many places at home to spread out a flat item at all, so I ended up on the kitchen floor. It's the only flat surface for cutting something large. My only other cutting-floor possibility would be the bathroom, which has a surprisingly big floor area, but you know, ew.

Barfley stays out because I put our kitchen chairs across the two entrances, and he is too big to crawl under and too big to go over, so it all works out.

After checking my bee samples, I spread out my material on the kitchen floor. I cut the pieces I needed for the dress and laid my scissors on the kitchen counter, then turned around to make myself a peanut butter sandwich for a snack.

Barfley took that moment to decide that the chairs were not, in fact, enough of a barrier to keep him from that luscious, peanutty goodness. He scrambled onto the chair seat, wagged his tail, and stared at me, a giant glob of drool dropping from his mouth and landing way too close to my silk pieces.

"Barfley, no!" I yelled, waving my hands at him. One of those hands was holding my sandwich, of course, and his eyes tracked it like a bee finding a giant pool of unguarded honey. I scowled at him and clutched the sandwich to my chest, then bent over to grab my silk pieces and move them to the counter. But I lost my balance on the way back up, and my arms started windmilling.

The sandwich arm flung out toward Barfley, who took it as an offering and lunged over the back of the chair. Then it was just like the movies: Time slowed WAAAY down. I saw him move, and I yelled and tried to move away from him. I was holding my silks in one hand and my sandwich in the other, and I reached for the counter for support. I saw the scissors right where my hand was going to land, and knowing those wouldn't be a good thing to grab, I let go of the sandwich, which started

to fall. Barfley grabbed it midair, sandwich bits flying
everywhere. In the meantime, my free hand landed next
to the scissors but didn't really get a good grip on the
counter, and my hand holding the silks flung out toward
the open window and the ledge with the bees on it.

There was NO WAY I was letting the bee samples
get away, so I dropped the silks as my hand went out
the window, and I managed to clamp my hand onto the
window frame and the bee box.

And the silks just fell on the shelf.

Except did I mention that the shelf is just a bunch
of slats next to each other? It's not solid. If it had
been, the silks would not have slithered like wet sheets
of pasta *between* the slats, falling down two stories
into the apartment compost bin. A compost bin that
was full of coffee grounds from the neighbors' morning
java, ketchup from someone's burgers, sauce from last
Friday's dinner with Grandma Parul, and grass and plant
cuttings.

I paused in shock, then ran downstairs, out the
main hall backdoor, and around to the alley where the
compost bin was. I didn't even think; I just jumped in
and grabbed the silks. But some slid down the side of

the bin, and the more I dug to get them, the deeper they went! I was up to my elbows in a week's worth of stuff that was supposed to be returned to nature. Stuff that *stains!* And STINKS.

When I pulled the silks out, I couldn't help it—I started crying. They were covered with stains and muck. There was no way they were going to survive this. I would have to start over. But I couldn't bear to throw them away yet. So I wiped my tears off with the one clean spot on the back of my left hand, went back inside, and put them in a plastic bag on my bedroom floor.

I don't have enough silk left to cut new pieces! Good thing I have donut money saved up, 'cause I'm going to need another time-consuming, and probably expensive, search at Britex. But I doubt I'll get lucky again.

When I went into the bathroom to clean up, I couldn't believe what looked back at me from the mirror.

If my assignment was to design a new costume for a garbage can, I'd be in *great* shape.

And then I saw a message on the counter that Mom wrote down from the Science Squad. Mari is asking Hannah and me to turn in our specimen reports during Monday, Wednesday, and Friday afternoons, which conflicts, of course, with Fashion Camp.

Great.

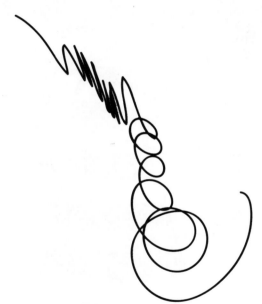

AMAZING DAY!

The most amazing thing happened at the Science Squad meeting today! Mari said we need to switch our schedule of when things are due so she can get them into the database. Her mom had some sort of meeting switch, and that messed with Mari's schedule. I must have crumpled when she said it, because Hannah patted my hand under the table, and even Kenny turned his head to glance at me.

I couldn't believe how many things we've had to rearrange. I started flipping through my calendar and barely heard anything that Mari was saying about our next steps.

When we went out for a break, Hannah asked me if I needed a Bee Good. I almost cried when she pulled one from her bag. Once again, someone is making me feel better with donuts. I'm sure there's something bad about that, but today, I didn't care. I hadn't seen a Bee Good in a while. Even though it meant I had more cash to replace my silk at some point, there is still a Bee Good-shaped hole in my life.

"How's your calendar?" asked Hannah.

"It's a *mess.* I get up early, stay up late, and still feel like I can't catch up. Maybe Mari is right—I can't do two activities and do them each well," I said.

"You know, I can take all the samples and record them for both of us, if that helps."

"What about your rock sampling? Don't you need time to work on those? I thought you were trying to identify every pebble you find in San Francisco this summer."

"I am, but keep in mind I am doing that for fun— no deadlines. I'll just switch tasks. They're rocks. They aren't going anywhere."

I laughed and ate my Bee Good. There must be something magical in the honey they use in them because out of nowhere, I got this idea. "Hannah, I'm so lucky to have such a good friend. But would you be okay working with someone else? Just for a little while? 'Cause I just got an idea. Where're Kenny and Jayden?"

My heart was a little fluttery by the time we got back in the meeting room. I told the group I had some scheduling issues. Mari sat back, crossed her arms, and smiled big at me, the jerk. And then I explained how I would be switching roles with Jayden. He would do morning collection with Hannah, and I would do evening light check and collection with Kenny. Mari was frowning by the time I finished. Keyarie leaned away from Mari, like she thought Mari was a bomb waiting to go off.

What a relief! If I do evening light check and collection with Kenny, I can move design time and data input to the morning. Then I'll have time to go to Britex if I have to do a last-minute change. And it doesn't hurt that the time is with Kenny. Thank goodness Hannah is okay with Jayden, and vice versa. She really is my best friend.

And then Fashion Camp was awesome too. Shonda is such a great friend! Today, I told her how my silk got ruined last night, and she gave me this big pile of solid black sateen fabric to cut a new dress. She said it just didn't inspire her anymore, and she was going to go and get something really colorful. I don't know what I would do without her in this camp.

I wish there was something I could do for her, but she told me if I sketched more on her designs, they wouldn't be *her* work anymore, they'd be mine, and she felt like that would be cheating. She's right. She also gave me back the books I lent her (yes, I remembered to give them to her the day after the day I forgot). I thought about her sketches and mine. Then I suggested maybe we could work together and pool our strengths— my designs and her eye for accessorizing and showing off the clothes.

She thought that was a great idea, and we could even plan our runway show together. Her only concern was if I had time to get it all done. I smiled and told her that wasn't going to be an issue anymore. Now I just gotta fix my designs.

Life is great!

Week . . . Uh . . . I Don't Know What, But It Was AWESOME!

This week was so cool!

I spent the early evenings with Kenny checking the lights! Actually, with Kenny and his big brother, Taishi, who drives us around. It's a nice change from walking and lugging bags around all morning with Hannah, although I do miss donut time with her. I feel almost *guilty* because I'm having so much fun!

Tai is a college student and a DJ, and he plays his music set lists in the car, listening for where and how he wants to do cross-fades and stuff like that. Tai is way older than us, so Mom and Dad were okay with me going out in the early evening to do the bee things with Kenny as long as Tai is our chaperone. Like we need one. I mean, we're not babies—we're *twelve*.

GET THIS: It turns out Kenny is a sounds-and-music

expert, and he actually helps Tai DJ when he does all-ages shows for the Parks Department. How crazy is that?!

Having Tai as our chauffeur/chaperone is the best! We get to listen to music and the noises and sounds that are added to the song. It's cool to think that Kenny made them. Kenny's not just cute, he's a SOUND GENIUS.

Like tonight, Tai played this song, and Kenny asked me to try to guess what this one sound was. I listened and totally could not figure it out. It was a sort of squeak that ended in a wail, like it was being stretched out. And it was in tune and on time with the music, so it sounded just like part of the song.

I finally gave up, and when I said that, Kenny smiled. Sooo CUTE.

"You really don't recognize it?" he asked.

"I really don't. What is it?"

"It's the squeaky hinge on the door from our meeting room at the library!"

And then I could hear it. It had been sped up and was at a different pitch, but I recognized it. And suddenly, all of Kenny's seeming spaciness and focus on weird things made sense to me. When he stares at lights or seems to be off in space, he's actually listening closely for sounds to sample.

When we check the lights, he hears things everywhere. Sometimes he points out what he's hearing, sometimes I ask him, and other times, I try and figure it out myself. It's *fascinating.* A whole other world! It's so cool that he's Mr. Science AND Mr. Music.

He told me that bees are the coolest creatures he's ever heard. They dance to communicate and make other kinds of noise besides buzzing. He showed me a video on his phone that he found of bees making a *whoop* noise when they are startled—like when they bump into each other in the hive. It's like a tiny hoot. So cute! He's thinking about using it in one of Tai's sets. And he said that bees are attracted to sound recordings of hives. He thinks there could be some way to use that to attract wayward infected bees to the lights at night.

Cute. Creative. Smart. He's so cool. He even offered to take tonight's samples and report them so that I can work on my fashion stuff. He's SO awesome.

Samples in my collection: 32

Samples showing infection: 0

Crushes on fellow Squad members: 1

Honeybees are the dancers and musicians of the insect world. When a scout bee finds food, she comes home and performs a specific dance to tell her sisters where she found it, vibrating her wings and waggling her abdomen. On the musical side, queen bees make sounds called "quacking," "tooting," and "piping." Workers make noises, too, including a "whoop" noise when startled.

Day of Runways

Today, Shonda and I started thinking about how to do our runway show. We are each working on our own designs, but I help her with her sketches, and she helps me with accessorizing what I've drawn. I still think my designs are *meh*, but at least when Shonda looks at them, she sees possibilities. Like today, she took a remnant of blue silk and tied it around the waist of my solid black dress like an enormous bow. It looked a lot better, but I still feel like the dress should bring something to the table.

We were thinking about doing a little extra to our fashion runway, like somehow we could make it dark and have lights along it, like the runways on *Junior Designer Showdown*. Then we could put chairs around it. My apartment is too small to host the runway show, and I just figured we'd do it at the workroom, but all the times are taken already. Luckily, Shonda said we could do it at her aunt's house, which will be big enough, and Shonda has a bunch of little camping lights we could use to light our runway.

We talked about what music to use. Since my style is more classical and hers is more contemporary and *eclectic* (new word I learned today—means a mix of different styles), we were having a hard time deciding. Seems like even the classical designers use edgy, more modern music in their shows, so I thought maybe I could check with Kenny and Tai and see what they might recommend.

I can't wait. It's going to be great. Now I just have to make those fashions worthy of being on a runway. Less craft project-y, more art and design-y.

The Worst Day. EVER.

The WORST possible thing happened today.

I knew that I had to work on my runway show.

I also knew the Squad would have to focus at some point on the "increase awareness" part of our ZomBee project. Hannah and I were thinking it would be a fairly basic thing, like posters or maybe filming a video. The Science Squad oath doesn't say anything about awareness, but we figured it's one of the things that makes all the difference in getting attention for your scientific questions. How can science be important to the world if no one shows people how important it is?

We talked about it a couple of days ago, and the Squad decided to do an evening event where we present our project and sell light traps. We'll invite everyone we know who might be interested. I got put in charge of finding the place to host it and lining up some kind of entertainment. Of course, Mari volunteered to be the person who presents the science portion. We had to talk her into doing other tasks that aren't science too. All it took was reminding her that we all want to go to Hawai'i and that wowing the Science Squad Assessment Team at this event would be just the way to do it. Then she was totally on board. In fact, she tried to add more to the presentation, but we talked her out of that.

I knew the fashion show would take a lot of work. And then this list for the awareness event wasn't exactly small. It was going to be a lot of time and effort.

But I never expected them to be on the SAME NIGHT an hour apart!

Yes, you read that right.

I didn't think it could get worse, but it did!

Today at Science Squad, we all compared calendars and discovered that the only date that everyone was available—and the assessors were able to come—was the same date as the night I have to do my runway show.

There is no way to get out of either one.

And I just can't pick one over the other.

WHAT AM I GOING TO DO?!

The (WORSER) DAY. EVER.

At Fashion Camp while we unpacked our stuff onto the worktable, I told Shonda about the Squad event being the same night as our runway show. I was totally dreading telling her. But Shonda took it really well. She said we'd find a way, and then she smiled and hugged me. It was comforting knowing that my fashion friend had my back. We weren't sure how I was going to get my fashions from my house to Shonda's aunt's house since the Squad event comes first that night. But we figured we'd work on it later and do our designs first.

I thought it was good that we knew our priorities, because apparently, I don't take my to-do list seriously enough. The zipper on my backpack still isn't fixed. Last night, Cute Kenny and I collected bees, and it was my day to take them home, but I forgot to unpack them, so they were still in my backpack today. I also had rocks in there that hadn't fit in Hannah's pockets from a few weeks ago. And I was so distracted by a noise that

Kenny found last night that I must not have sealed the bag of bees. Although none of this would have been a problem if I had just paid attention to what I was doing at Fashion Camp today.

Shonda and I had laid out our materials on the table and were trying to decide what changes to make to which pieces. Shonda had a really beautiful yellow top that went with a skirt that she didn't like.

"I have an idea," I said, reaching for my messenger bag where my sketchbook was. But what I actually grabbed was the backpack, and when I hauled it up, Hannah's rocks shifted the weight of the bag and flung the bag of bees (that wasn't sealed) onto the worktable.

Only it wasn't just bees.

I *finally* got a sample that was infected.

Fly larvae and dead bees scattered all over the table.

Well, not the table, exactly. More like onto my carefully laid-out dress. And some landed about three centimeters from Shonda's fashions, wriggling. And did I mention that Shonda had her head really close to the fabric, inspecting some stitches? I froze.

She looked sideways.

"OH MY GOD! Are those dead BUGS!?" yelled Shonda, snatching her designs. Everyone in the room came over to look. "Blech!" she yelled. "YUCK! Some are moving! Maggots were almost on my stuff!" She shivered and grimaced and clutched her fabric to her face.

As others inspected the situation, noses were wrinkled, faces were made, and people skulked away in disgust. All I heard was "Ew, ew, ew." And "They're dead!," "No, those white wormy things are alive!," "Why did she have that in a baggie?," and "Whoa, that's just weird."

"They're just dead bees," I said, panicking. "Well . . . and their parasites. It's for a science project . . . I . . . uh . . ."

One of the counselors came over and asked if I could clean it up, and if I knew if they could infect people.

I told the counselors that the bees did not infect people. I wanted to sweep the bees into the trash can and pretend it never happened. I had to bite my lip to hold back the tears of embarrassment. I managed to hold my tears in as I pulled out some tweezers and carefully collected the bees and larvae one by one and put them back in the bag, then sealed it. I was so upset, I barely even registered that I had an infected sample. Although both infected and noninfected are important for the research, I'd been secretly hoping for an infected bee. Now I was so mortified, it didn't matter, and I actually thought about throwing them away.

And to make matters worse, Shonda finally stopped shuddering, turned to me, and said, "Okay, I'm sorry about that. I just really don't like squirmy things. But, I . . . I think maybe we should change our plans for the runway show, I mean, I can't . . ."

I held up my hand and stopped her and swallowed hard. I knew what she was going to say. I grabbed my stuff and left the room. In fact, I flew down the three sets of stairs, left the camp, and went home early. Tears managed to eke out on every block on the way home.

We're at the point in our project at Fashion Camp where we don't get instruction from the counselors anymore. We are just working on our final designs and shows. We don't have to do that at the workroom unless our parents insist, or we need help or are working . . . (WAH!) in a group.

So, I don't ever have to go back.

I am utterly down. I am a total nerd again, and I will always be known as a nerd. Science will be all that I have. But that's okay. I don't need Shonda. I have Hannah. Science is great, and I am science girl. But even though it's great, it doesn't exactly get you invited to dances and parties, which might be nice someday, especially if I could bring Kenny. Guess I'll have to settle for collecting dead bugs with him. Great.

Samples in my collection: 31
Samples showing infection: 1

Day of TRAITORS, Part 1

Apparently, "Secret Schedule" is a bad name for a file. Especially when your digital files are stored alphabetically, because this puts it right next to the "Sample Schedule" file.

And that makes it very easy to accidentally click that Secret Schedule file and upload it to a public folder on the shared folders list for your Squad. I mean, anyone can do it, just click, click, clicking away. Especially if you are in a hurry or, oh, I don't know, TIRED.

"Secret Schedule" practically requires a fellow twelve-year-old to open it up and look inside. Like it's the sacred duty of every sixth grader to check out anything that might result in A) candy, B) secrets, or C) both. And while my schedule may not have had A), I basically put up a neon sign that said "SECRETS INSIDE! All who can read! Step right up and SPIN THE WHEEL to SEE WHAT YOU GET!" Sort of like in a horror movie, when you tell the main character not to go in that old, empty house, but they are drawn to it like bees drawn to big purple flowers full of pollen in a sunny corner. No bee can resist that.

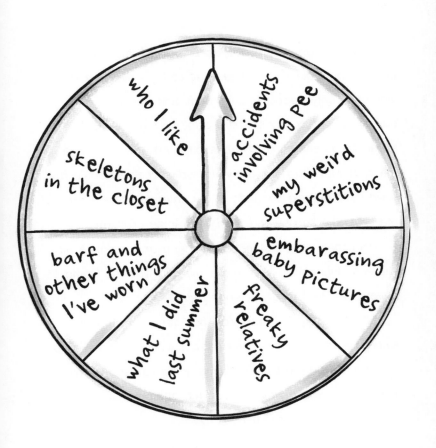

So I shouldn't be surprised that someone found my secret schedule.

And it should not surprise me that it was MARI who found it.

And used it against me.

Keyarie came up to me as I sat with my head down on the table during the break at today's meeting. We were the only people in the room. She doesn't usually say much, but today she had a lot to say. She looked so guilty as she blurted—oh, excuse me, *confessed*—to me that Mari had found my not-so-secret schedule and used it to create conflicts in my calendar. She even told me that she had helped Mari with some of them.

In other words, Mari had planned and created all the schedule changes to make me quit Fashion Camp so I would focus only on Science Squad!!

She's totally twisted! Mari has been my nemesis ever since we were eight. In the past, I would have believed it if you had told me that she was going to use information like that to find a way to beat me at something. But this is a new low, even for her.

Then I remembered that Mari really wants our Squad to go to the Hawai'i convention. The fact that she once said she's never traveled out of the Bay Area may have something to do with it. But she made my life a nightmare. I THINK I MIGHT ACTUALLY HATE HER!

Keyarie said she knew it had gone on too long when I didn't want any donuts today (why is everyone so obsessed with my need for donuts?) and that she was so sorry that our meetings moved to Tuesdays because of her dance class. It had been Mari's idea, and Keyarie'd gone along with it. Then she said this was a fight that Mari couldn't win, because I'm "so strong and determined." I know she just said that so I wouldn't be totally mad at her, but it did soften the blow.

I could feel myself getting hotter and hotter, like there were tiny chimneys behind my ears. When Mari came back before everyone else, I ~~asked~~ DEMANDED to know if it was true that she had created all of the crises and changes in the schedule. All the panic and stress and late nights and early mornings and confusion. I yelled that I'd left bees in donut shops, and larvae had fallen out of my backpack at Fashion Camp because of her!

She smiled almost evilly. I don't really know anyone I would describe as "evil," but this is the closest that I have seen. So, you know, *almost* evilly. I wouldn't have been surprised to see horns sprout out of her head and a pitchfork appear in her hand. Okay, maybe not the pitchfork.

So then she said, "Yes, in fact, I have been. How did you finally find out? You're so clueless, there's no way you figured it out on your own."

I didn't mean to, but I looked at Keyarie, who shrunk against the wall. I'm sure Mari already knew and was just being dramatic for effect.

Mari scowled at Keyarie. "I'll deal with you later, you traitor." Then she turned back to me. "You do realize I had to do this. It's what's best for the group. You didn't listen to me when I said we all have to be 110 percent committed to the Squad! And as our leader, I have to make hard decisions to make things work for all of us, not just one of us." She tilted her head back and stared down her nose at me with a complete air of superiority. "And you are all about being just one."

"I am *not* 'all about being just one'!" I said, standing up. "And you are *so* not our leader."

"I AM the leader, and you ARE all about you! You put years of our hard work in danger because of your need to be Little Ms. Fashion. Well, I'm glad you finally came to your senses, and now you can totally focus on science. If you don't, I will personally find a way to make sure that everyone—not just us, but everyone in the Science Squad organization, especially Ms. Char—knows that you let the whole team down. That it was all *your* fault. Oh look, here's the team now."

Just then, Hannah and the other members of our Squad returned.

Hannah immediately came and stood by me, a look of concern on her face, and Kenny came to my other side. I had my own personal squad of awesome.

I was ready for a throwdown.

Note to both selves:

Never label anything "secret." It will ruin your life.

.

Day of TRAITORS, Part 2

So, sometimes the only way to know who your friends really are is when you are confronted with a really icky situation, like Queen Mari telling everyone that you might be the reason they don't get to go to Hawai'i.

Mari said to everyone (oh wait, not *everyone*, since Ms. Char still hadn't come back yet) that I was a selfish jerk who was going to ruin our chances of winning the trip to Hawai'i because I was betraying us all and doing some dumb fashion show thing.

"You stole my calendar and planned for me to fail!" I said in defense. "You rearranged times and meetings so that I would have to skip or switch things around. You did this on purpose!"

I saw Hannah's jaw drop.

"You failed us on your own, trying to do too much!" Mari screamed back.

I felt that heat building behind my ears again, but before I could respond, Hannah spoke up.

"I think it's cool that Raksha can do the fashion thing and the bee thing at the same time. You wish you had half the creativity she has, and if it wasn't for you messing with the schedule, this wouldn't be an issue. Even so, I only had to enter stuff for her a few times."

Oops. Thanks, Hannah. I turned to her in disbelief. I know she was trying to help, but did she realize that in Mari's view, that made me look like an idiot who couldn't always do her own work? Did she forget that Mari would grab onto anything less than perfect and make it sound like a total weakness?

"Ha!" said Mari. "*See?* Her best friend had to cover for her. You can't do both, Raksha. I don't see what the problem is—the bees and science come first. Fashion is shallow and *irrelevant* to the real world. I can't believe you don't get that. You're a smart girl. You can't be both of these things." She conveniently left out any response to what Hannah had said about her messing with the schedule.

"I would have been fine if you hadn't gone and changed the schedule all the time," I said. At least, I think I would have been.

119

"Sure, go blame the schedule. I bet you didn't even do half the work when collecting and reporting. Is that how you won the science fair? Come to think of it, are you doing the work now? Or is your *boyfriend* doing it all for you?"

Kenny was silent, and so was I, at first. I mean, he wasn't my boyfriend. Was he? I liked him, but I had no idea if that was even in his realm of reality. A boy, who was a friend, who I like—that's all he was, right? I didn't risk looking at him because I was afraid that if I did, I would see that he was making a face or something that would show that being my "boyfriend" was gross.

"I am not his girlfriend," I said quickly. "We're fellow Science Squad members, trying to get our project done. And he has occasionally done an entry for me, but not all the time. We are both working hard. Now you can stop messing with the schedule. Your little game is over. No more changes."

"No more changes necessary because I made my point! Now all that is left is for you to be a good worker bee and do your job and help us get to Hawai'i." Mari crossed her arms with a satisfied look on her face.

Then Ms. Char returned, and we all fell silent and sat down.

"Guys, I have some bad news," she said. "The venue you wanted to use for your presentation just called me. They will still be finishing their remodel on the day of the presentation. You'll have to come up with another place or idea."

Mari didn't miss a beat. I can't believe what she did next (well yes, I can, since she is the middle school equivalent of the God of Chaos).

"Oh, that won't be a problem. We were just talking about how great Raksha is at parties and fashion and that sort of less serious part of our project. She has plenty of time and could totally find us a new venue and music and all that kind of nonscience stuff, can't you, Raksha?" She nodded her head like she was answering for me.

What could I say? Mari didn't create this latest issue, and it *was* my job to find the place. She had me cornered in front of Ms. Char. If I said no, I'd look like I wasn't a team player. And that was the whole point of the final project—to show that we could do science stuff on our own while also demonstrating teamwork.

I found myself nodding at everyone, like I was Mari's little puppet. Kenny just glared at Mari. He was probably mad that she had called me his girlfriend and was totally grossed out. Collection this evening was going to be totally awkward.

I had to sit there with all that anger simmering below my fake smile through the rest of our meeting.

When we got out, Hannah and I went to the steps outside together to wait for her mother to pick her up.

"I was going to bring you a Bee Good today, but I didn't have a chance," said Hannah. "If I'd known that Mari was behind all of this craziness in your life, I would have brought the donuts for sure. Not to feed you, but to smear all over her face and leave her by a beehive!"

I said it was okay because it wasn't Hannah's job to feed me donuts. Then I said, "And it is also *not your job* to defend me, I can do that myself. You made me look BAD. That was really not helping, Hannah."

Hannah just sat there, looking surprised. My cranky side just kept at it. I feel bad now, but at the time, I just let it roll.

I went on, "You know you have to be more *careful* about what you say. I mean, if you hadn't said something on that first day, Mari wouldn't have found out about this at all. And then I wouldn't be in this mess."

"WHAT?!" she yelled. "This is not *my* fault! I shouldn't have said something because, apparently, I can't do anything right? What a joke! You are the most ungrateful friend ever!"

"I'm not ungrateful. I just didn't need your help!" I spat back.

"You know what? You're right. You don't need my help. You need, like, a professional's help!" Hannah said.

"Yeah? Well, that's not you!" I said.

"Fine! Then I won't say anything else or try to help you ever again," Hannah said.

I should have just said I was sorry right then and there, but I didn't, and I still regret it. All I did was walk away.

Day of TRAITORS, Part 3

Night collection with Kenny was totally uncomfortable. We barely said anything to each other. He didn't point out any cool sounds or talk about what musical work he was doing. A few times, he looked like he wanted to say something, but then he just gulped a lot and looked ill. Probably getting grossed out about the idea of having a girlfriend.

Or worse, did he think he really did do most of the work? Maybe he took Mari seriously?

I decided I should let him off of the hook. Better to cut this friendship off now myself than to have another friend cut me off like Shonda or Hannah.

I told Kenny that I was going to go back to doing work on the bees during the day, now that Mari wasn't going to keep changing the schedule.

"Wait, so you're giving up on fashion? She wins? After all that garbage she said? I didn't think you were the quitting type," said Kenny.

"I'm not *quitting*. I just think it might be better to do things separately. I don't want her to think that, you know . . ." I was going to finish with "that you do all the work and I do none," but he cut me off.

"Yeah. Don't let her think what she said today is true," he said, looking at the ground. "Don't let anyone think that," he mumbled.

"Wait, you think that you . . ." Did he really think that he did all the work? What a jerk!

"No, I don't think . . . um, what are we talking about? Oh, never mind," he said. "It's no big deal. You can probably switch back with Jayden if you want."

We got in the car with Tai and rode in silence until we arrived at my apartment. "I'll see you tomorrow or at the next meeting, I guess," he said as I got out.

"Yeah, whatever," I said, and I slammed the door and went into my building.

Mom somehow had read my mind and brought Bee Goods home tonight. I was only able to take one bite. I told Mom and Dad I was going to bed early. That way, nothing else can go wrong today because I am ending the day now.

The Day the Universe Spoke to Me

I think maybe this has all been for the best. I have already gone through two pillows. They are all soaked with my tears, but it's a small price to pay for the knowledge that maybe my experiment didn't work.

Maybe I should just face the fact that Mari is right. I can't be both things. I mean, the bees and larvae spilling all over the worktable at Fashion Camp wouldn't have happened if I hadn't been doing the science thing. And having to deal with nasty rivals wouldn't have messed up my schedule if I had been just doing fashion and not science.

Now I really do have to choose.

But there isn't much to choose from. Both things feel ruined for me. Fashion Camp and my bid for popularity is over since the one person who could have helped me doesn't want to work with me anymore.

And my friends in science don't want to have

anything to do with me, either. Which is no big surprise, given how I acted.

I think I might choose not to do either. I tried sketching some design changes earlier, and I totally have creative block. I didn't even know that could happen. And I tried calling a bunch of different places to host the presentation and places to do the runway show (not that I expect many people to come). I can't find a place for either one. The universe is definitely trying to tell me something, and it's "DON'T BOTHER DOING THIS!"

I thought I was mad at Hannah for even getting me in this mess in the first place, but it's not her fault that I uploaded my schedule to the shared folder where Mari found it.

I miss Hannah-Moondew-Sunshadow. I miss our morning walks and our donut stops and figuring out her new name. And I miss Kenny already too. I hear interesting noises, and I wonder what he could do with them in a song.

And I miss Shonda. I don't know how I'm going to face her and her popular friends at school. I hope she doesn't tell them about "bee girl." Wait, no. I guess I'd be "dead, squirmy things girl." That's even worse.

I guess now I'll have to miss them all, since none of them will probably want to talk to me ever again. And they won't have to, because I am pretty sure that I am done with both activities.

I'll start over. I don't have to be science or fashion girl. Maybe I'll try something new, like a sport.

Nah. I won't go that far.

The Day the
Universe Barfed Stuff
All Over My Floor

This is my second day in my room doing nothing. It's the weekend, and I have nowhere to be. I've been hiding out from my parents, who usually want to spend all weekend with me. I told them I'd had a rough week and wanted to just get some rest and hang out around the apartment. They were fine with that.

I've finished off the Bee Goods that Mom brought home—and the sour belts I had stashed. What am I gonna eat now? I tried sketching again. Nothing useful. Just doodles of bees and fashions, all sort of mixed together on the same page.

Then I stuck this journal in my messenger bag and tried to read a book. But Barfley kept nosing some noisy, crinkly thing in the corner of my room. That dog never gives up, especially if he thinks there's food lying around.

I got up and pulled him away and grabbed the plastic bag he was trying to open.

It was my damaged silk pieces. I'd totally forgotten them. Mother nature hadn't, though. They were all covered with some hideous moldy stuff, in addition to the stains they already had. Red and yellow merged with black and green in a nice medley of *nastiness*.

I gagged and threw them in the corner, where they knocked over my backpack and messenger bag, neither of which were closed, of course. Stuff fell out all over, covering half the floor and intermixing. WHY DOES THIS ALWAYS HAPPEN TO ME?

I was going to separate it all and put it away, but instead, I stopped and looked at the mixed mess of my life. I got down on my hands and knees on the floor and must have looked like a total brain donor as I pawed through everything.

The first Bee Good donut bag from the day Hannah gave me the bee ring was on top of the mess, and then my journal open to the stuff I wrote from when I started working with Kenny. They made me think of Hannah and her tea channel and rocks, and Kenny and his sound and music projects. I saw my sketches of fashions for the bees next to sketches of my final looks for Fashion Camp, my examples of light traps, and my enormous to-do list.

All this stuff felt useless now that I no longer had any friends. But it did make something stick in the back of my mind. I just don't know what it is. It's hiding and won't come out. I'll figure it out later. I left everything on the floor where it was.

One thought does keep coming to the front of my mind, though.

I miss my best friend.

I think maybe I could at least be friends with Hannah again, even if I can't fix anything else.

A big apology is in order.

Note to science self:

A bag of wet, moldy silk makes an interesting noise as it lands after being thrown across the room.

Day of Apology

I went to Hannah's house, because this had to be done in person. Face-to-face. I would have brought Bee Goods if I thought I could show my face in the donut shop again. I could have used one on the way over to Hannah's house. It's a bit far away, but the long walk gave me lots of time to practice my apology. Which went something like this:

"Hannah, (or whatever amazing natural name you are using right now), I am a nincompoop. My nincompoopery knows no limits, and I am sorry. The universe told me to come apologize to you. You tried to help me, and I appreciate that you tried. Please forgive me for not recognizing how supportive you are."

I thought it was pretty good and sounded really *mature* and like I was as sorry as I felt. I was hoping the word *nincompoop* would make her laugh, at least.

And it worked! Hannah started crying, and she told me that she was sorry, too, and that she never meant for my life to get so rough, and if she had to do the argument with Mari over again, she would. And this time, she wouldn't say ANYTHING unless I asked her to. I told her that really wasn't necessary.

I told her I'd stopped collecting with Kenny. She thought I was wrong about what he thought of me, but what does she know? Marc Fisher in our math class has made moo-moo eyes at her since second grade, and she doesn't believe me.

I told her it didn't matter anyway. It was done, and I was now available and willing to help with the morning collection again. And we agreed to meet at the next morning shift (I guess that's Monday) for a collection run. She also told me we had another infected sample. I never thought I'd be so excited about larvae again, but I was.

We went inside, and Hannah (now Starshine) asked me to help her with a little makeover. I told her we had to figure out a way to allow her to collect and bring home rocks. I tried again to convince her to wear pants, and she refused until I pointed out the Zen of yoga pants and athletic leggings.

Unfortunately, there's no room in those sorts of

clothes for rocks. So, I worked on redesigning her bag. While I was sketching, she watched for a bit, and then she said, "I really think you should still do both. Look at how good you are at this."

"Both? Oh! You mean fashion and science. You know that means a lot to me, I'm just not sure I can make it all work—there's just so much to do."

"I think if anyone can, it's you."

We sat there in silence as I stitched new pockets on the outside of her bag.

We picked out a couple of outfits together, and I finally introduced her to a pair of espadrille sandals. They will be very cute on her. I hope she gets that those are for dressy occasions (well, her version of dressy, anyway). Given her "grab whatever" method of dressing, I don't have a lot of hope. You can offer a horse a clean bucket of filtered water, but if it wants to drink from the bacteria-infested lake instead, you can't stop it.

And you know what, if I want to be the world's first scientist/fashion designer, who can stop me?

I think Hannah might be right. I mean, Mari is going to leave me alone, now that she's made my schedule

such a mess that she thinks I can only do science stuff.
But maybe I can still do both.

Now, I just gotta figure out how . . .

Note to fashion self:

Offer to help reorganize Hannah's closet and make a
lookbook for her.

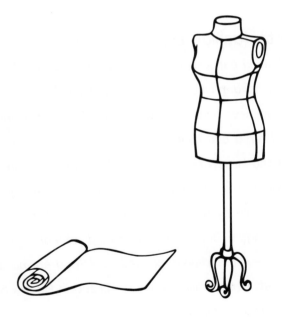

The Day the Universe FINALLY Explained Everything

Note to fashion self:

Freaking out and running away from a ZomBee is way, *way* harder when you are wearing boho chic.

On my first hunt back with Hannah this morning, I reached for a bee that turned out to be very alive. The second the tweezers touched it, it hopped up and flew in a ragged line over my left shoulder. I froze, figuring the bee would fly away and I would just catch it when it landed again. But it veered toward Hannah—I mean Starshine—who shrieked, jumped back, and sprinted down the street, arms flailing in every direction like a startled, tree-hugging octopus.

As she inhaled (deeply) for a second scream, her fresh-flower headband fell forward into her mouth. She choked and stumbled, spewing out carnation and daisy petals like a fountain as she tried to keep running. Her cute espadrille (yes, she wore them) came off the front of her left foot, and her run became more of a loping, kicking gallop as the shoe flopped around like a canvas-covered brick tied to her ankle.

When she started sneezing, she veered a little too far to the left and tripped, flopping into a flower bed, where she lay hacking up plant parts.

If that had been me, I would have gone into hiding for weeks. But since it was ~~Hannah~~ *Starshine*, she sat up, wiped the various bits of leaves and flowers off her lips, and started laughing.

"I'm okay, and I STILL LOVE NATURE!" she said as she shook the remnants of her headband out of her hair. "Hey, that's a cool rock."

My best friend is the *best*. But if she models in my runway show, I'm going to make sure she's in flats. And pants.

Note to science self:

I wish the bees had little signs so we could tell a regular-but-confused worker bee from a ZomBee. It would be great if you could. ZomBee hunting would involve a lot less screaming, shrieking, and fumbling, and way more science-ing.

Summer To-Do List:

OLD:

27. Still gotta figure out where I'm going to host my runway show.

28. Oh yeah, and figure out where to host the Science Squad presentation too.

32. Get the rest of the bulb cages for the light traps to be sold as fundraisers, and start assembling them.

33. Figure out why my designs are still just so . . . meh.

NEW:

139. Develop a boho outfit that involves less problematic shoes without the wearer going barefoot (yuck).

140. Convince Hannah, Starshine, or Whatever-name-she-picks-next-week to start wearing red flowers, since red is the least attractive color to honeybees.

141. Now that I know that Kenny helps his brother DJ on weekends, I should find out where he is playing next. I still want to see him perform, even if he thinks I'm

a loser. Maybe I'll just go in disguise. Big sunglasses cover everything and look chic too!

142. Find a way to clone myself so I can get all this done, because there is no way this is all coming together. TOGETHER! Like all the stuff on my bedroom floor! THE UNIVERSE HAS SPOKEN!

27 + 32 + 141 = 200

I have 200 percent solved my time problem, but no time to explain, I gotta go!

P.S. Come to think of it, I've solved #33 too.

Another Day of Apology

So, how do you apologize to a friend who is a boy but not a "boyfriend," and who is totally grossed out by that thought, but you have to talk to him again because you A) kind of miss hanging out with him and B) need his advice and suggestions? And maybe he thinks he did most of the work and thinks you are an idiot and a quitter?

I figured out the best apology I could come up with. Last night after dinner, I walked to the beginning of the route I know Kenny takes to check the lights at night.

When I saw Tai's car come around the corner, my mouth went dry. What if Kenny just hates being around me? I really need his help to make my whole plan work, but more importantly, I don't want him to hate me.

He got out and looked at me, then leaned into the car and said something to Jayden and Tai. Then he came over to me, his hands in his pockets.

We stared at each other for a moment, and then

I told him that I was sorry that I was so mad before, and that maybe he was right and he had done most of the work, and I'd *never* meant for that to happen.

He looked at me, and his jaw dropped a little. My stomach twisted. He must have thought I was a TOTAL IDIOT.

Then he said, "Oh wow, uh . . . that's not what I thought at all. I only did that stuff for you once. It was no big deal. I was just pretty mad at Mari for saying . . . um . . . that fashion and music are nonscientific things." He blushed.

I think I was in shock. I couldn't say anything out loud. It was like when a DJ does a stand-alone record scratch and there's a pause before the music winds back into a cross-fade. I tried to form words, but my head was all tied up, thinking that I was the HAPPIEST PERSON ALIVE! He doesn't think I am gross! Yay! But somehow, I just couldn't let that out. I still didn't want him to think I wanted to be his girlfriend—that's too weird, right?

Then I remembered my apology gift for him.

"I, um, keep hearing all these cool noises and sounds all over, and I made a list of where and what time I heard them, in case you want to go record them and sample them for Tai's sets." I handed him the now-sweaty piece of paper I'd been clutching in my right hand.

Kenny's eyes lit up, and everything felt right again. He said, thanks and then it got awkward because Jayden and Tai were probably watching us from the car.

"I was wondering if you might help me with a special project involving sound," I said. "I mean, it's for the bees. Maybe we should ask Tai and Jayden to listen to this too."

I explained my plan to all of them very quickly because I had to be home before sunset.

Kenny and the others said YES! Now I just gotta figure out a few more things.

Note to science self:

Boys and what they think versus what *you* think they think would be an interesting thing to study.

A Lot of Days of Work

In our Science Squad meeting today, Mari looked surprised when she realized everyone but her and Keyarie were sitting on one side of the table. Why does Keyarie hang out with her? There's no way that Mari is fun. Good thing Jayden will keep my secret plans from those two. Keyarie is okay, but I don't know if I can trust someone who is close to Mari.

I have, of course, removed my calendar from the shared folder, but knowing Mari, she would have made a copy anyway. But she doesn't care now, because she has me *right* where she wants me.

Which is right where I want to be.

I loved the look on Mari's face when she was about to write our remaining tasks on the whiteboard for the awareness fundraiser! I raised my hand and nodded my head just like she does. And I said I already knew what I was going to do to display the light traps and that Kenny, Jayden, Hannah, and I were working on music, entertainment, and refreshments. She seemed very suspicious but couldn't really say anything with Ms. Char saying how great it was that I was volunteering.

Ha! Mari looked like she'd eaten a thousand lemons compacted into one lemon-filled donut without sugar.

And she practically fell out of her chair when I said, "I think that Mari has worked very hard on this project and should focus on taking time now to really practice her summary of all of our hard work and the science behind everything we have done. We need to really make a good impression if we are going to win the trip." I gave her my own Cheshire Cat smile.

Is there such a thing as being unnerved? I don't think you can actually be de-nerved, but if there was such a thing, it would totally describe the way that she looked. Then I could see the wheels turning under her brown curls. She was probably thinking that I gave in and this was her chance to totally dominate and take as much credit as possible for everything. Then I *swear* she snuggled into her seat, like a little kid getting ready for the special movie they have been waiting for.

"Don't worry about anything," I said. "We'll take care of all the setup and preparing your podium and getting the lights all ready. Like you said, yours is the most important part." I couldn't resist one dig: "And you won't have to touch any of the specimens. We'll take care of that too. We don't want a repeat of the aquarium."

Mari grimaced and then actually said, "Thank you."

Finally, she is off my back!

It was the best meeting we've ever had, but now I am off to a meeting of my own that does not involve Mari. Hope this all works out.

145

The Day I Thought ZomBees Ate My Brain

ZomBees have eaten my brain.

I'm tired and can barely think, again! But this time, I'm so excited that I just keep going and going. I suppose the large amount of caffeine I drank in the three iced teas I've had today may have something to do with that. Or maybe it's the fact that I have to pee, like, every fifteen minutes—that'll keep you awake!

I hope this all works! There are a lot of moving pieces. There are so many, I had to move my to-do list to a separate piece of paper.

I am so glad that I have Hannah and Kenny and no schedule issues. Our secret meeting the other day went really well. I think it's because we decided to keep Mari completely out of the plans.

Hannah brought teas she had specifically blended to use as the refreshment at our presentation. She was pretty excited about one of them because it involved adding rocks to the brewing process to flavor the tea.

I won't upload anything to the shared folder that gives any information about my plans for this fundraiser and fashion show. I can't believe I didn't think of it sooner. All it took was spilling stuff. Oh, and thinking of all my friends and how they all manage to be a bunch of different things at the same time.

But I'm on track now and ready to go. There's just so much to do, but I think that I can do it.

On my fashions, I have this black dress and these beautiful bell sleeves I want to add on, but I am not sure how to do it. I want to attach them to make them removable. I could ask for help from the Fashion Camp counselors, but I'm not sure I can go back to that great white loft of embarrassment. I am still just too *mortified.* I probably shouldn't be so worried. I'm sure some of the other people in that camp have been in situations where they were super embarrassed. Besides, most of our time at this point is spent out of camp anyway. Maybe there wouldn't ~~bee~~ be (ha, I wrote "bee"— wonder if that means something?) that many people there.

I am dealing more with construction than sewing. I twiddled around with snaps and Velcro, but they really didn't work. Maybe ribbons will be the thing. I need a trip to Britex. *Oh yes, a trip to Britex will do very nicely.* And I have all that hoarded Bee Good money to provide a budget for buying. Hmm.

So, to give my brain a break, I switched to working on spray-painting the bulb cages. Luckily, we have a decent rooftop work area on our building, or that would never have happened.

At least I have the other fashions done, and Hannah agreed to be my second model.

I just hope she doesn't trip.

ZomBees will not eat your brain, and neither will the larvae of a zombie fly (*Apocephalus borealis*). The zombie fly was already known to infect other insects, particularly bumblebees and wasps, before the discovery that it infects honeybees too. But so far, it is not known to lay eggs in or on human beings.

The Day ZomBees REALLY Ate My Brain

So, here's proof that ZomBees have eaten my brain. I realized I needed a third model for my runway show. And since I'm not really comfortable talking to Shonda at the moment (because that would require showing up at the workroom and feeling totally judged), I had to look at my other friends, which right now, are just the Science Squad. Which pretty much left me with Keyarie. I thought, *Why not?* She's graceful from all those years of dance and looks like a normal human being. You know, like, she has a head, a torso, and two arms and two legs, so at this point, that's good enough!

I am ashamed to admit that I actually used her guilt about helping Mari to my advantage. Wait, no. I guess I am not really ashamed, because you know what? She owes me. When I told her I really needed a third model and that she would be a great one, I also mentioned that I was on such a tight schedule now that Mari had made my life a nightmare.

Um, yeah. With facts like that, of course she said, "Yes, of course, oh my gosh, whatever you need, I'd be glad to help."

Then I told her the plan, and she was even more invested in it, because now she knows a secret that Jayden thought he was keeping from her.

She came over for a fitting today, and hanging out with her wasn't bad. She's kind of one of those quiet people who, when you finally get them to talk, are actually very interesting. Get this—once she got to dance for one of the princesses of Japan at this international dance expo her dance group went to. I didn't even know that Japan still had a royal family and that there was a REAL-LIFE PRINCESS. How cool is that?

I also learned that the only reason that Keyarie hangs with Mari is that Hannah and I have each other and Mari is the only girl left. She said Mari is easy to get along with, but she does have some moments where she is just a little intense. I had to bite my cheek to keep from yelling, "A *little* intense? Ya think?" Instead,

I tried to focus on the other part of what Keyarie was saying, which is that Hannah and I had each other. I pointed out that there's always room for other friends.

My only concern was that Keyarie might get weak and tell Mari, which would spoil everything. But now, after talking to Keyarie, I think it'll be okay.

Invitation Day

Today, I sent out the invitations for the ZomBee Hunters Guild event and the runway show. I gathered the names on the list I had from our meetings and my list of contacts for the project. I added a few names, and since I was in charge of both lists, no one would notice.

I even invited the owner of Nuts for Dough, Mr. Rod Sapperstein. I'm crossing my fingers that he will be very understanding when I tell him that I accidentally let those bees out in his shop. Maybe after seeing that it happened because I am involved in a very important scientific process, he will be okay with it. He must like bees. After all, he named a donut after them.

This week, the invitations from the other Fashion Camp runway shows all arrived. I'm debating whether I should go to any of them. I don't have a lot of time.

Maybe I'll just go to Shonda's show. But then again, I bet she thinks I'm gross, so maybe not.

The Day I Became a Spy

So, I went to Shonda's show.

Her aunt's house was perfect for her runway. She lives in one of those older San Francisco houses that is super tall and narrow, with Victorian architecture, similar to the famous "Painted Ladies" houses. It's the kind of house everyone thinks we own in San Francisco but that very few people actually live in. I can't think of one person I know (other than Shonda's aunt, now), who lives in one of these houses.

Shonda's runway came down the stairs, which were in the middle of the house, and through the living room, library, and dining room. People were spread out all over the first floor. It was a little crowded, and no one could really sit, which worked out just fine for me. I decided to go at the last minute. It was noisy, so they didn't hear the door open and close when I came in. I hid behind the taller people by the door at the end of the hallway. Plus, I wore my giant sunglasses so that I wouldn't be recognizable. And I didn't bring my backpack, just a small black purse.

We were only supposed to show three outfits, but she showed seven great looks that were really well accessorized and put together. Then, at the end, she pointed out that her clothing designs were pieces that she kept intentionally very basic. And she was right— they were pretty simple. She told us how she was really frustrated with her designs until she realized she really liked styling outfits more than designing clothes, and that Fashion Camp gave her the knowledge to figure that out. So, her focus was on how to combine multiple pieces for a whole look. I was really glad she finally found her fashion niche, and despite trying to stay hidden, I clapped really loud.

I'm glad we didn't work together, because I think that she would have spent most of her time trying too hard to design, and she never would have realized her strength in styling.

I had a hard time getting out the door, even though I was right next to it. Everyone was shoving and rushing to get out and go off to the next show. Suddenly, I heard Shonda's voice down the hall saying, "Hey, Raksha! Wait! Raksha!"

No way was I ready to talk to her. I bolted for the door and managed to squeeze out and sprint down the block without being caught.

When I got home this afternoon, I went over all of my plans and double-checked everything. I hope my show goes as good as Shonda's.

"Nervous" doesn't begin to describe how I feel about tomorrow's events. Everything is done: the fittings, the collecting, and the prepping. I have all my pieces in place and all my other stuff ready to go. I just hope nothing goes wrong.

I'm just hosting a runway show in the middle of the ZomBee Hunters Guild Awareness Fundraiser. I mean, what could possibly go wrong?

The BIG Day of Bees, Part 1

I came early and met the rest of the group at the restaurant to set up. Did I mention the restaurant actually has a yard out in back, like a whole fenced area outside with grass and everything, and it usually does small concerts in the summer? I'd asked Kenny if he could think of places for us to do the event that would allow everything we needed, and when he and Tai talked, they thought this was the best choice. Luckily, the owner owed Tai because he had done a special performance for her daughter's sixteenth birthday.

Mom and Dad hung out at a table in the back where we had stacked our printed event programs. Mom pulled out her laptop and started working. Dad settled on a chair and pulled out his phone. I bet he was checking in on my cousin Raj's cricket match down in Cupertino, which we (thankfully) had to decline to attend because of my presentation. But hey, at least Raj is getting some exercise, unlike my parents. They really need screen-restriction time.

The restaurant let us set up the outdoor yard however we wanted. We put two rows of light traps in the center of the yard from front to back, making a path. Then we put Mari's podium down at the end of the light path, and we hung white sheets as a curtain behind it that could also serve as a projection screen. On either side of the path, we put all the audience chairs at an angle so they were facing both the path and the podium.

We had everything in place when Mari arrived. I felt kind of bad for her (not *too* much, though). She actually looked nervous and was sweating like crazy, even though it was a cooler night. Keyarie suggested she go practice in the restroom to feel better, and Mari didn't argue. Then we put all the fashion stuff behind the curtains, including a pop-up tent as a changing room. I stayed back there, laying out my fashions as people arrived.

Eventually, it was time to do the presentation.

We all took our seats next to the podium. Kenny arranged the lights to spotlight the podium, but the light traps were dim and only lit a small patch around them on the ground, so I couldn't see who all came and sat down. It felt like a big crowd based on the noise and murmurs. I tried not to think about who all was out there.

Ms. Char got up and did her part, talking about the Science Squad organization and our history as a group and how we'd all made it this far. She showed a slideshow of our four years of effort, and she teared up for a moment. Then she introduced Mari.

Mari got up and started talking. She was very serious and managed to be calm and cool and collected, even though I knew that she'd thrown up in the women's restroom because I'd heard all these retching noises and the only person who had come out was her.

She went on and on about how important our work was and went over the numbers and what we found, how we found it, etc. She described in detail how to assemble the light traps, which (little did she know) was going to come in really handy for the crowd to understand the entertainment part of the presentation. Then she thanked each of us from the Squad, like she was a beauty pageant contestant and we were her support team. As each of us was done being mentioned, we fled the stage to go to our next tasks. I was last.

"And I would especially like to thank," she took a deep breath, "Raksha Kumar for the *softer* side of the project and her nonscientific ideas on how we could bring awareness to the plight of our beautiful San Francisco bee population. I've learned that being a great leader means that you should recognize the resources you have available to you, and I am happy to say that I saw that Raksha could be the mind behind the fun little entertainment portion of the project. This next part of our presentation should really speak to those who are not as science-minded and make this scientific project accessible to the layperson."

I paused. For a moment, I was surprised she was handing me a compliment, then I realized it wasn't one, *not really.* She was trying very subtly to make it sound like she was the wise leader who was smart enough to put me in charge of doing this part and that my part wasn't science. She was totally taking credit for my work in a way and yet putting it down too! And come to think of it, she was putting the "laypeople" of the crowd down as well. Was she just so rude that she didn't even realize she was doing it? Probably.

Rather than outrage, all I could think was *Wait 'til she sees what I have up my sleeve.*

She stepped down from the stage and came to me, then turned her back to the crowd. The second only I could see her face, she grabbed my elbow, pinching it a bit.

"This better be good," she hissed. Then she left me to go take her seat.

Instead of the podium, I walked to the front end of the presentation area, between the two rows of lights. I still couldn't see the crowd beyond the low lights, but that was probably a good thing. They say if you are nervous speaking in front of a crowd, you should imagine your audience in underwear. But I think the fact that all our parents were in the crowd somewhere would cancel out any humor. Instead of *Ha, ha, I'm so relaxed,* I'd be thinking, *EW!! Oh my GOD!! EEEWWW!!*

I said, "Hi, I'm Raksha Kumar, and I spent the last few months hunting ZomBees. I have also spent those months working on fashion designs at Junior Fashion Camp." There were sounds of surprise from the audience, and at least two gasps. That must have been Mom and Dad.

I went on. "Both of these things are really important to me, and I thought they should both be a part of something bigger, so tonight, our entertainment is a ZomBee-themed fashion runway show. I call my three-piece fashion collection the ZomBee Hunters Guild Party. My inspiration for these designs was all the things we learned about bees during our Science Squad project. If you turn the pages in your programs, you can read the description of my inspiration for each outfit. So, yeah. Here they are."

Somewhere in the darkness, Mari was probably sitting there with her jaw hanging open. I admit I was disappointed that I couldn't see her face. I'm sure she looked something like this:

With a nod at Kenny and Tai, I went back by the curtains. The yard started to fill with thumping music, and the lights (light traps) brightened on the "runway." Then they started turning on and off in sequence, matching the beat, just like Kenny said he could program them to do. A thrumming hum provided the background for the dance song Tai played, and every now and then, there was a little *whoop* that I knew was the bee *whoop* sound that Kenny had put in.

The sheet "screen" parted in the middle, and out came Keyarie in a cream silk top and a two-part skirt. The skirt had a basic black A-line skirt as the underskirt and then a top skirt made from separate wide strips of ombré cream that faded into blue silk. The bottoms of the strips were covered in what could be interpreted as a flower-garden pattern around the bottom. Of course, it was my stained silks, all repurposed. I found that when I washed the silks, the nasty mess from my dumpster dive and the mold growth (gak!) had actually stained the fabric into an interesting, almost-floral pattern on the ends. This was my "bring on the bees" skirt. It was blue with flowers—how could any bee resist it?

I don't think Keyarie was totally on board with being a model until I showed her the outfit. She'd thought the top skirt was so great that it should be used in a dance recital. So, her payment for her silence and being a model is that she gets to keep the outfit.

Keyarie spun and twirled her way down the runway, performing a little dance, just like she said she would. It was supposed to look like a scout bee who found food and was trying to let the hive know where it was.

Leaving Keyarie turning in time to the music, I went into the tent, passing Hannah who was running out in the second outfit to wait behind the curtain for her turn. I knew Hannah demonstrating the second outfit would give me enough time to put on my final outfit.

I managed to finish dressing and returned to the side of the curtain in time to see Hannah come out. Her outfit was a mostly red peasant top and skirt, complete with flat sandals—no espadrilles! Hannah's modified bag with pockets was there too. She turned, and the skirt flared out, revealing leggings underneath. This was my "hide from the bees, so they can't see ya coming" outfit.

She stopped halfway down the runway and pretended to check a light trap and empty it into a zippered baggie, which she then tucked into one of the Velcro pockets on the bag. Watching her, I got the idea to modify my own bags with some sort of Velcro, since I never seem to remember to fully close anything. And we know what that has led to . . .

At last, I took to the runway, wearing my black dress that was anything but basic. I'd added a broken hexagonal pattern made from gold ribbon on the fabric on top, subtly hinting at a honeycomb. Then, at the end of the sleeves, I'd attached light-trap bulb cages spray-painted black to be the "bell" sleeves. They were cut open on both ends (cut nice and *wide* open—not like a mailbox opening, I might add) so that my arms could go through.

For an accessory, I carried a black bucket bag, literally made from a small bucket covered in black fabric with two wide black ribbons tied in a bow as the handle. When I reached the end of the runway, I unclipped the cage from one of the ends of my sleeves. Then I removed the funnel from my funnel-bucket "purse" and grabbed the light bulb socket part that I'd stored inside. I attached everything together and plugged the whole thing in to the extension cord I'd laid at the end of the runway. It was a light trap, just like the others we'd put out! When I turned it on, the whole crowd said, "Ooooo!"

Then I stood up between Keyarie and Hannah, who were posed on either side of the runway and said, "Ta-DA!"

Because I didn't know how else to end the show.

People took pictures. Applause, whistles, hoots, and lots of clapping filled the air. Some people came up to us and started shaking our hands and telling us how moved they were. They told us this whole presentation was a great way to bring knowledge of this latest risk to honeybees.

I looked around, but Mari was nowhere to be seen. The last I'd seen her, she was heading for the refreshment table, but when I looked there, all I saw was Mr. Sapperstein staring at me, like he'd just been told something very important.

ACK! It's dinnertime. Gotta go.

The BIG Day
of Bees, Part 2

When you approach a donut store owner to make an apology for letting a swarm of bees loose in his bakery, make sure you have all the facts ready. And if you are lucky, maybe your archnemesis isn't totally mad that you put a fashion show in the presentation, and she didn't tell him everything.

I went over to Mr. Sapperstein and introduced myself and thanked him for coming.

He smiled at me but still looked like he'd just been told that bees don't make honey.

He said, "I got this invite, but I didn't really know *why* I was invited until I saw your stuff tonight. Now it makes sense! I know you. You and your friend always come in and eat at least two or three Bee Goods and unicorn teas." He waved at Hannah, who was showing the people at the other end of the refreshment table the varieties of honeys she'd picked to go with her own special brew of tea. "You must have seen the poster I put out saying that I was going to donate 50 percent of the proceeds from the sales of Bee Goods to the Help the Bees Fund, and you remembered! And hey, didn't you leave your backpack in the store about a month ago?"

Oh well, time to confess. It couldn't be worse than admitting I am idiot to my friends. So, I said, "Yeah, that was my backpack."

"Oh, my goodness," he said. "That was one crazy day, with all those bees coming from who knows where, and people running out, and all the screaming. I'm not surprised you left your backpack. Were you okay? Good thing you had that tag on the underside of the strap, or I wouldn't have figured out who to call."

WHAT? He had no idea that the bees had come from my bag? I thought for a moment about confessing anyway, but it seemed like it would be such a bummer for him. He looked so excited that someone had seen his sign and cared. This meant Mom and Dad couldn't find out that the bees came from my bag either, and that's a good thing, since I'm sure that if they found out I was letting ZomBees loose in the restaurants where we eat, they would never let me out of my room again. And I don't think I can spend too much more time in my room anymore, especially now that I know it's the *perfect* environment for growing MOLD SPECIMENS.

Nope, I was definitely not saying anything more on that!

I said, "Yeah, well, you said it: It was a crazy day. I was, uh, following the bees. Thanks for getting my backpack back to me. I love bees, but this project was a lot of work, and it helped to have your delicious donuts there the whole way." Okay, *most* of the way.

Then, get this, he said, "Hey, maybe you and your group could do a party like this at my store, and I could supply Bee Goods. We could even sell a light trap and Bee Good coupons in a pack to customers and donate the proceeds from that."

I was so touched by his interest in helping the bees! That just made those Bee Goods seem sweeter. I said, "Wow, that sounds really cool! I'll talk to the group about it!"

"And from now on," he said, "one Bee Good a day is on me. And you know, come to think of it, we could use some new aprons and T-shirts for the bakery. Maybe you could design some for me?"

WHAAAAAAT?! My urge to jump up and down *almost* overcame my need to not be embarrassed, but thankfully, it didn't.

"That would be great! I'll just have to figure that out with my mom and dad." OH MY GOD! THIS IS AMAZING! My first fashion-design customer!!

Mr. Sapperstein said he'd be in touch and walked away, heading over to get some tea from Hannah.

Then Shonda came up to me. I was so surprised she was there. All of the fashion kids were there, actually. They probably were hoping I'd make some sort of mistake or spill something creepy and gross on someone. They all came up behind Shonda and were checking out my three fashions with what I hope was admiration.

"That was AH-MAZING!" Shonda said and then tentatively hugged me. I just stood there, stiff. I still had memories of betrayal and total embarrassment in my head, but then she blurted out, "You ran out of my aunt's house before I could tell you, and I didn't know your phone number or e-mail, and you didn't come back to camp. I wanted to tell you that what I was *trying* to say was that my aunt is allergic to bees, and I wanted to make sure that you didn't bring any of your bee stuff when we did the runway show. Looks like you did just fine without me, though. Wow!"

The other kids murmured similar things—I mean, minus the whole explanation—but things like "Wow!" and "Great job!" But all I could think was that I'm not a total science dork, and Shonda doesn't think I am gross grub-girl!

I totally hugged her back and said thanks as the rest of the fashion crowd patted me on the back and talked about how creative my designs were. They thought it was really cool that I mixed the fashion in with an important issue. One girl even said that she thought that if we'd had a competition, I would have won, and a bunch of the others agreed. I think some were disappointed that there were no gross things to look at, but when I mentioned they could all go check the traps for bees, most of them practically ran, tripping over one another to get to the runway and check to see if we had any results.

Okay, maybe that's not exactly how it happened.

Maybe that is just what I wished would have happened. But two of them DID go look out of curiosity, and four of them bought lights. I noticed they bought the lights that had the same bulb cage I had used on my dress.

And then Ms. Pence came and shook my hand and told me how impressed she was that I'd applied real-life utility to my designs, and she wondered if I was going to join the advanced program next summer. I was so startled, all I could do was nod. She nodded back and said, "Great!," then walked over to Keyarie to inspect the skirt.

With the other Fashion Camp people spread out all over the yard, it was just me and Shonda. Shonda said that Hannah and I should come and hang out with her sometime this summer, and we could work on fashion stuff! When I told her Hannah really wasn't into the fashion thing, she said she remembered that but was hoping Hannah wouldn't mind being our own personal live model and dress form. I told her Hannah wouldn't care, as long as we let her pick up rocks—and we fed her donuts.

Shonda laughed, and then she said, "I'm SO glad

that you came to camp. I really liked being able to talk to someone who would get the idea that you are so into something, that you'd spend the entire summer working on it. I figured you were really into science, and a science geek can totally understand an art geek, right?"

"Of course!" I said.

"Oh, and you and Hannah are going to hang out with me at school this year, right? My friends think I'm insane for not spending every moment this summer hanging at the pool, but I've seriously loved being able to spend all this time on fashion. It would be nice to have a real fashion friend this fall."

I was stunned again. I couldn't believe Shonda thought this. She thought our different sides would mean we could *relate* to each other, and all I did was focus on the *differences*. And she wanted to hang out at school?! YAAAAYYY!

"Yeah," I said, trying to be cool. "We should totally hang out this year."

And then she hugged me and went off to talk to Tai and Kenny about the music.

I looked around and finally saw who I really needed to talk to.

Mari.

The BIG Day
of Bees, Part 3

Mari was standing alone next to the end of the runway, holding a cup of Hannah's tea and staring at the podium.

I went to stand next to her and stare at the podium too. I didn't know what to say to her.

Ms. Char came up to us and said, "I think that your runway show made *quite* the impression on the judges from Science Squad nationals. Kimuchi Ihito is a really picky judge, and she couldn't stop talking about how your ideas are exactly what science needs. She actually said they are a way to bring interest to scientific issues and research that may not have had an audience otherwise. You had a good presentation planned, but this? It made a good presentation *great* and may have been enough for you guys to get that trip to Hawai'i! Good job, you guys!" She patted us both on the back and walked away.

All I heard in that was "Fashion is going to save

science, and great job, Raksha." I wondered what Mari heard.

I turned to her and said, "Uh, you did a really good job on the presentation part." Why was I so nice to her? Well, I thought she *did* do a good job talking about the science, and I might have been feeling (just a tiny, itty-bitty bit) guilty for not telling her about our plans.

She didn't turn to me but just kept staring at the podium. Finally, she said, "You did a really good job too." She was silent for a few more seconds, and then she said, "I can't believe you still did both Science Squad and Fashion Camp, even after I tried to make sure you would only do science so we could win. And now we're winning because of your fashion thing." She turned to me, her eyes narrow. "How'd you do it?"

"We all have different things we do outside this group, you know. Hannah has her tea channel, Kenny has his sounds and DJing, Keyarie has dance. We just had a few meetings and—"

"Without me," she interrupted.

"Yeah, without you." *Duh.*

"How did you know that this would be what would put us in the lead for the trip?"

"I didn't. I just had to do what I had to do. I had to give our project all of me. I realized that I spent too much time trying to keep the science and fashion separate, and I just ended up holding back on both sides. What I should have been doing the whole time was both, together."

"And that got the attention of Kimuchi Ihito and is probably gonna get us to Hawai'i. And I almost messed that up."

"Um, yeah."

She looked at me, expressionless, like a brick. I couldn't tell what she was thinking.

Then she said, "I should start gymnastics again."

WHAT?! Where the heck had that come from?

She went on, "I quit when I first joined Science Squad, but I really miss it. I thought you could only really be good at one thing at a time. All I've had is science."

I couldn't believe it. I was a part of some grand realization on her part?

"But now I know I can totally do two or even more big things. Because it must not be that hard if you can do it." Then she stared at me for a moment, raised an eyebrow, and walked away.

UGH! And I was just beginning to think she's human. Some things never change!

The Week of Marine Biology, Mynahs, and Goddesses

I have not written for a very long time because I am, once again, very busy.

Busy lounging on the beach!

Everything smells better in Hawai'i. Flowers, food, the ocean. Even the grass smells warm and welcoming, its scent saying, "Everything is good, and everything will always be good. There are roads still left to travel and questions that still need be asked and results to explore." That grass scent says a lot. It's very encouraging, for a smell.

The other thing I love about Hawai'i? No one cares if I am two different things. Indian and Chinese, fashion and science—everything can coexist peacefully. A lot of people here have a lot of different parts that make them who they are. They are all pretty mellow about being a blend of things. Probably because it's too hot to think of anything other than being cool. I really love it here.

And why am I here?

BECAUSE WE WON!

The ZomBee Hunters Guild was selected to represent the Bay Area at the national convention! We do our presentation in three days. Mari has gone into overdrive, insisting that I be both fashion girl and science girl because it will help us win nationals and maybe go to the International Science Squad Convention. It's in Antwerp. I don't know where that is, but Mari is dying to go. Her ambition (or is it a travel bug?) knows no limits. She even offered herself up as a model. I not sure whether that is a good thing or a nightmare.

Then again, I think I already have a great design in mind for her outfit for a presentation.

I'm learning to play the ukulele in a class taught at the hotel. Kenny thought some of my strumming was good enough to add to some of the music Tai is using in his next Parks Department concert. Hannah and Keyarie are taking the same ukulele classes, but he didn't say that to *them*. I guess I'm *special*. But what does that mean?!

I got to go snorkeling today. I love it! It's fun following the fish and seeing wildlife underwater. I wonder what it takes to become a marine biologist? I mean, I like bees and all, but maybe I would really love being a marine biologist. I could even be the scientist who designs apparel and gear for other marine scientists! Maybe I could design a whole line of special wet suits just for marine biologists who want to stay under for extended periods of time and blend in to study the underwater world. I'm pretty sure the fish know something is up when a person-shaped thing drops in the ocean clad in solid black. Why aren't wet suits made in different shades of blue? Couldn't the color vary based on what water you are in? Or maybe you could put seaweed patterns or coral patterns on them to blend in?

Hannah stays mostly on the beach because she's convinced that I will be eaten by a "large, toothy fish." I'm pretty sure she just means "shark." She may not like the water, but she sure is enjoying the rocks.

We got to go out and look at the different kinds of lava rock, and she was in awe. She even said she might focus on volcanology (that means the science of volcanoes!) someday. But now she is afraid of touching anything because she does not want the great Hawai'ian goddess Pele to be mad at her. Apparently, Pele will be angered if you take any lava rock from the islands.

Hannah is so paranoid about even the sand stuck on the bottom of our shoes that she suggested that when we get on the plane home, we go barefoot to avoid offending the goddess.

I think Hannah's new name should be Petra StoneStare, High Priestess to the Great Goddess Pele.

Kenny is in sound-geek heaven and finding tons of different noises to add to songs. I learned from him today that the word for "mynah bird" in Hawai'ian is *piha'ekelo,* which means "full of sound." He thought that was beautiful, since he was fascinated with all of the noises they make. I didn't tell him that when I looked it up in a Hawai'ian dictionary to see how to spell it, it also listed *manu-'ai-pilau,* which means "filth-eating bird."

I saw some bees today, and I thought maybe we could set up light traps here and see what we collect. Wouldn't that be a great excuse to stay a little longer? Ms. Char didn't go for my suggestion, although she seems content to lounge by the pool, drinking freshly squeezed tropical fruit juices. Her favorite is POG, which is short for passion fruit, orange, and guava.

Shonda would love all the fashion inspiration and material I'm getting from this place. Yesterday, I went to a fabric store that specializes in Hawai'ian fabrics. I mean, there were just hundreds and hundreds of bolts of fabric in there, all waiting to be made into all sorts of things. I should send Shonda postcards for fashion design inspiration.

Speaking of mailing things, I should probably mail this journal home, because it's full now. And I don't know if I'll have room for it in my luggage with all of the stuff I've collected (no rocks, just fabrics) to bring home.

Only one problem.

I'm afraid of the mailbox in the hotel lobby.

It looks really hungry.

What are zombie bees? A zombie bee (ZomBee) is a honeybee infected by a tiny parasitic fly known as the zombie fly (*Apocephalus borealis*).

What's happening? Fly larvae grow inside the bee, eating it and making the bee stagger around. Scientists also think the infection causes some bees to leave their hives at night. These freaky behaviors led to the name "ZomBee." The zombie fly is known to infect other insects, but honeybee infection appears to be a new phenomenon.

Where is it happening? Since the first known infection was discovered in San Francisco in 2008, infected bees have been found by citizen scientists in several places around the United States and Canada.

Why is it important? More data about the infection is important because we need honeybees to pollinate our food crops. Without animal pollinators, 75 percent of the world's food plants would have a hard time producing high-quality fruits, vegetables, nuts, and other products that we eat. Beginning in 2006, honeybee colonies across the United States started suffering from Colony Collapse Disorder (CCD), a syndrome where most workers of a colony abandon their homes and disappear. No one knows why it happens, but infection by the zombie fly may be one of many elements causing CCD.

In the Field

Picking up snacks for a pet praying mantis doesn't usually lead to hunting zombies.

Dr. John Hafernik is a professor in the Department of Biology at San Francisco State University (SFSU) in California. It is his job to study creepy-crawlies. He's an entomologist, and now, he's also a ZomBee hunter.

When Dr. Hafernik gathered some dying bees near where he works on the SFSU campus, he thought they'd provide a delicious meal for a praying mantis he was keeping. Instead, he discovered a new threat to honeybees: the zombie fly.

After noticing that his mantis meals were infected by zombie fly larvae, he and his colleagues got to work collecting infected honeybees, called "ZomBees," around San Francisco. Before his discovery in 2008, the zombie fly had not been known to infect honeybees.

To find out just how big the problem was, he started the ZomBee Watch Project to get help collecting ZomBee samples around North America. It can be hard to recruit people to help, though. Because, as he says, larvae bursting out of bees to pupate is "kind of gruesome."

Glossary

Colony Collapse Disorder — *A problem happening to honeybees, where most workers of a colony abandon their homes and disappear. No one knows why it happens, but it may be caused by a combination of several situations that are not good for bees.*

entomologist — *A scientist who studies insects.*

hive — *A nest or home for honeybees, sometimes also called a beehive.*

larva — *The second stage of life for insects that go through four stages to become adults, sometimes also referred to as a maggot. Usually, the four-part life cycle includes egg, larva, pupa, and adult stages.*

light trap — *A trap that uses light to attract insects.*

parasite — *A living thing that uses another living thing for survival. It is a one-sided relationship that is only good for the parasite.*

pupa — *The third stage of life for insects that go through four stages to become adults.*

thorax — *The middle section of an animal body. On a bee, this is the area where wings and legs are attached. It is located between the head and abdomen.*

ZomBee — *A honeybee infected with zombie fly eggs or larvae.*

zombie fly — *A tiny parasitic fly that lays eggs in other insects to provide a food source for the larvae. The eggs hatch into larvae that consume their host from the inside, causing the host to behave in weird and strange ways.*

Selected Bibliography

"Honey Bees: Heroes of Our Planet." *The Honeybee Conservancy*, thehoneybeeconservancy. org/2017/06/22/honey-bees-heroes-planet. Accessed August 15, 2017.

"Pollinator Protection: Colony Collapse Disorder." *United States Environmental Protection Agency*, www.epa.gov/pollinator-protection/ colony-collapse-disorder. Accessed August 15, 2017.

"What are Zombie Bees?" *ZomBee Watch*, www. zombeewatch.org. Accessed August 15, 2017.

About the Author

Amanda Humann lives in Seattle, Washington, where she writes and draws stuff for a living. When she isn't doing those things, she enjoys games, puzzles, cooking, ~~studying weird plants and animals, asking questions, and blowing stuff up~~ science, and eating candy. Her honors for writing include the Young Adult Library Services Association's 2014 Quick Picks for Reluctant Young Adult Readers (a division of the American Library Association).

About the Illustrator

Arpad Olbey is an illustrator veteran and art director of his art studio in London. He works with paper, pencils, and paints, or digital high-tech equipment, depending on the project. His wish is to combine his experience and technical knowledge to deliver the best that his creativity can give to audiences.

Hatchling Hero:
A Sea Turtle Defender's Journal

by J. A. Watson

Illustrated by
Arpad Olbey

Hardcover ISBN:
978-1-63163-160-3

Paperback ISBN:
978-1-63163-161-0

Clarita Rosita Santiago Romero hasn't made many friends since moving to North Carolina last year. But that changes when she joins her local Science Squad and simultaneously gets sucked into a quest to defend a sea turtle and her eggs from poachers. But how much impact can a group of kids have on one sea turtle's life?

AVAILABLE NOW